Shadow Lane
Volume 7

How Cute Is That?

by
Eve Howard

CCB Publishing
British Columbia, Canada

Shadow Lane Volume 7: How Cute Is That?
A Novel of Spanking, Sex and Love

Copyright ©2009 by Eve Howard
ISBN-13 978-1-926585-48-2
Second Edition

Library and Archives Canada Cataloguing in Publication
Howard, Eve, 1953-
Shadow lane : volume 7: how cute is that?, a novel of spanking, sex and love /
written by Eve Howard – 2nd ed.
ISBN 978-1-926585-48-2
Also available in electronic format.
I. Title.
PS3608.O82S537 2009   813'.6   C2009-904900-7

Cover and interior artwork by Tarsis: www.briantarsis.com

Shadow Lane Volume 7 was originally serialized in *Stand Corrected* magazine,
Copyright © Shadow Lane 1997-1999, and was first published by Blue Moon in
2003, Copyright © Eve Howard.

Publisher: CCB Publishing
               British Columbia, Canada
               www.ccbpublishing.com

Dedicated for

F. T.

David and Hope

Shadow Lane

Volume 7

How Cute Is That?

ℰℭ

Contents

David and Brooke

Chapter One

Matchmakers

On Thanksgiving Day, instead of dressing a turkey, Laura Random was dressing a video set for the taping of an interview with the first paying client of Matchmakers, Inc.

Laura's subject, Dr. Julian Honeywell, took the chair provided for him in front of the camera, unbuttoned his grey suit jacket and waited impatiently for Laura to adjust her soft lights and gels.

"Would you like to look over my list of questions?" she asked him, adjusting his position slightly.

"Surprise me," he replied cynically. He was a handsome six-footer, with dark hair and eyes, who while meaning no harm, radiated that particular mixture of arrogance and irritation common to doctors.

"Very well," said Laura, adjusting her focus, consulting her script and hitting her record button. After a short pause she asked, "Julian, where were you born?"

"Manhattan."

"And how old are you?"

"Thirty-eight."

"Where were you educated?"

"Columbia and U.C.L.A."

"Would you state your profession?"

"I'm a cosmetic surgeon."

"Where do you practice?"

"Beverly Hills."

"Do you own your own home?"

"Several."

"How did you vote in the last presidential election?"

"For the winner."

"Have you any religious affiliations?"

"None."

"Do you have any hobbies?"

"Skiing, biking, surfing, travel and film."

"What's the most exciting city you've ever visited?"

"Amsterdam."

"What's your favorite film?"

"The Red Shoes."

"Do you smoke?"

"No."

"Are you willing to date a girl who does?"

"Sure."

"Do you drink?"

"Now and then."

"Do you use recreational drugs?"

"No," he lied.

"Do you object to girls who do?"

"No."

"Have you ever been married?"

"Once, shortly. It didn't work out."

"Did you ever spank her?"

"Once, shortly."

"Are you looking for marriage?"

"Not if I can possibly avoid it."

"Why is that?"

"Marriage is boring."

"Are you open to a long term relationship?"

"Yes."

"How long have you been into it?"

"I spanked girls as early as kindergarten."

"Are you strictly dominant?"

"Yes."

"Would you consider dating a switchable woman?"

"I'm not sure what that mean."

"That means a woman who gives as well as receives."

"Oh. Sure, so long as she doesn't want to switch with me."

Laura thought this was going better than she expected. He seemed frank and reasonable.

"Could you take a few moments, Julian, to describe the characteristics of your ideal play partner?"

"Certainly. She should be late twenties to around my age, slim, fit, well-educated, career-oriented and very submissive."

"Do you mean sexually submissive or personality-wise?"

"Both, I suppose."

"And why is that?"

"I hate arguing."

"What kind of scene are you looking for?"

"Spanking, costumes, role playing and sexual servitude."

"Sexual servitude?" Laura sounded more surprised than he thought reasonable.

"The type of woman I'm looking for should enjoy pleasing me," he replied, a bit stiffly.

"What kind of corporal punishment are you interested in?"

"Over the knee spanking, paddling, strapping, whipping and caning."

"Have you any experience with any of these?"

"Lots."

"And how did you achieve this?"

"A few ex-girlfriends and ...others," the circumspect surgeon replied, remembering that most of his experience had been with professional submissives at B&D clubs.

"Would you describe yourself as pragmatic or romantic?"

"Both."

"Will you require absolute obedience from your submissive?"

"Yes," said Dr. Honeywell's penis.

"Would you make a girl change her dress if you didn't like it?"

"Yes."

"How about the color of her hair?"

"Only if it was awful to begin with."

"Do you expect to make all the decisions in the relationship?"

"Not all."

"Most?"

"That depends on the circumstances."

"Do you consider yourself even tempered?"

"Sure."

"Patient?"

"Within reason."

"Strict?"

"I can be."

"Severe?"

"At times."

"What's the object of a spanking to you?"

"Discipline."

"How about foreplay?"

"Sure."

"How important is it to you that the girl be turned on by the spanking?"

"I wouldn't be here if that wasn't an important factor."

"Are you willing to accommodate your lovers or must they accommodate you?"

"Since I'm looking for a submissive the answer to that should be obvious."

"How do you feel about compromise and negotiation?"

"I'm not entirely opposed to compromise, but in a true D&S relationship it shouldn't be necessary."

"So, you'd prefer a classic D&S situation to a simple spanking relationship?"

"Yes, I thought I'd made that clear."

"What sort of controls do you intend to enforce on your submissive?"

"I don't know. That depends on the degree of control she seems to require."

"You wouldn't, for instance, lock her in a closet if she disobeyed you?"

"Certainly not!"

"Have you ever spanked a girl until she cried?"

"A few times."

"How did you feel about that?"

"I enjoyed the hell out of it."

"How about the girls? Do you think they enjoyed it?"

Dr. Honeywell perceived he was being baited. Though, in point of fact, every girl he had ever made cry was a B&D player whom he'd spanked at a club for allowance and he had no way of knowing how any of them had truly felt about being punished so severely.

"Please stop filming," he said. She complied and the next moment he was standing a foot away from her with an unpleasant look in his penetrating eyes.

"Laura, whose side are you on here?"

"Excuse me?"

"This interview seems designed to vilify me."

"I'm just asking the questions that occur to women into spanking when they're considering a partner."

"But I understood that most of your female subscribers were submissive."

"They are."

"Then why do I perceive an undercurrent of challenge, and even hostility in your line of questioning?"

"I don't know," she equivocated.

"I suppose you're anything but submissive yourself," he snapped.

"Me?" Laura fell back a step.

"If you have such a problem with dominant men why did you pick this job?" he demanded.

"I don't have a problem with dominant men," she replied with amusement.

"Then why don't you ask me some good questions, like how I plan to spoil the lady I pick?"

"Okay. I will," she agreed timidly, eager to neutralize his pique as quickly as possible.

"Good!" he said and took his seat briskly with a glance at his watch.

"Are you in a hurry Dr. Honeywell?"

"No, why?"

"Because after we get done here you're scheduled for a strategy planning session with my partners and me."

"I hope it will be a more positive experience than this interview has been so far."

"You know," she said, focusing her Nikon on his face to snap some stills for the club's catalog, "I'm only asking the questions, you're providing the answers. If you think you're coming off like a male chauvinist, it's likely that some women will too. I do think it would help if you smiled, though."

Julian attempted to ignore this recommendation but she was far too attractive to stay mad at for long, particularly in her cardigan, tweed skirt, stack-heeled oxfords and anklets.

"Great smile," Laura said encouragingly, snapping several portrait shots. "Now do me a favor and fold your arms. Go back to being stern." Laura took her shot. "Thank you. Now may we continue taping?"

"Yes," he said, unable to remember for a moment why they had stopped. The fact that he had been powerfully annoyed by Laura Random only minutes earlier suddenly eluded him, though he remembered as soon as she got the camera rolling again.

"Julian, would you spoil your submissive?"

"I'm looking for a girl to spoil. I enjoy going shopping and live only a couple of blocks from Rodeo Drive." Now Dr. Honeywell smiled again.

"And I suppose that for the right girl you'd throw in a nose bob?"

"Cut!" cried Julian in exasperation. Laura hastily paused her camera and peeked out from behind it.

"Is something wrong?"

"I don't appreciate that kind of sarcasm. Particularly not at my expense. Now, are you going to start behaving like a professional?"

Laura stood up to him with a pounding heart and shakily replied, "I apologize if I offended you, Dr. Honeywell. I see now that my lightheartedness was inappropriate."

Julian looked skeptical.

"I'm very sorry." She hung her head meekly. Then she peeked up at him. "Can we finish the taping now?"

"Haven't you got enough?"

"I have pages more questions."

"You're kidding."

"I offered to let you see them."

"I'll take two more questions. This is far too nerve wracking to endure any more than that."

Laura set the camera rolling again and glanced through her questions. Then she smiled and plunged in once more.

"Julian, could you relate to a woman who entertained anal-erotic fantasies?"

"Actually, as a physician, I have a state of the art examining room and am extremely interested in meeting women with medical fantasies. I would guess that any woman who was anal erotic would be a natural candidate for enemas. I can certainly administer them and enjoy doing so."

"Finally, Julian, what's your favorite way to make love?"

"I'm flexible, but have a partiality for taking ladies from behind."

Some twenty minutes later, Patricia Fairservis and Marguerite Alexander sat with Julian in Patricia's lighthouse reviewing the tape. Both were smartly suited and alert as they considered their first wealthy client's possibilities. Laura busied herself making coffee and pleased Julian by serving him.

"Well, I see no problem here," said Patricia enthusiastically. "You're a great catch."

"Laura seemed to think I was conveying the impression of being chauvinistic," he told them, giving Laura a glance as she sat down.

"Well, naturally your requirements for a classic submissive are going to lose you some possibilities, but not a significant number," Marguerite informed him.

"I understood that most of your female subscribers were submissive," he said, becoming irritated all over again.

"Oh, they are," said Marguerite, "but to varying degrees."

"We can always edit the tape to make it a little more innocuous," Patricia suggested.

"I suggest we try it as it is," said Marguerite. "If Dr. Honeywell knows what he wants, he might as well get it."

"What part would you suggest editing?" Julian asked, unsure as to whether he was hating or enjoying confronting the three of them like this.

"The part about sexual servitude," Patricia promptly replied.

"I disagree, Patricia," said Marguerite firmly. "It's best if this requirement is stated up front. Otherwise you might run into an awkward situation on a date."

"I think the remark has to go," Patricia firmly stated, "unless you want to come off sounding B&D sleazy."

"Okay, I'll take your advice," he told Patricia, only slightly wounded.

"Wonderful," said Marguerite.

"So, what happens next?"

"Well," said Marguerite, "there are several options open to you at this point. The first is to simply run your ad and photo in our catalog for as many months as it takes for you to attract a compatible mate. With all you have to offer, one or two issues should do it."

"Tell me about the other options."

"Well, you've just made a video. You might want to order a supply of your tape from us, and then have it on hand to send to the more tempting respondents to your ad."

"Sure. I'll order a case if you think it will help."

"You won't need more than a couple of dozen," murmured Marguerite, aware of what a prize Dr. Honeywell was.

"Anything else?"

"There is one other thing," said Marguerite, "but I don't think you'll need it."

"Tell me."

"Private introductions," she replied.

"Private introductions?" he was intrigued and excited.

"Research is expensive and of course does take time," explained Marguerite, "but we can find you a brilliant submissive."

"Guaranteed?"

"No. But you only have to pay if we achieve success."

"Find me someone like Laura Random," said Julian when Laura slipped out of the room with the coffee tray. Marguerite and Patricia exchanged a smile.

"Now girls, don't get too excited," Marguerite cautioned after Julian had departed. "You know he'll be inundated as soon as his photo ad comes out. He may never have recourse to a personal introduction."

"Meanwhile, he gave us the authorization to get busy," Patricia reminded her.

"That's true," said Marguerite.

"He won't feel satisfied unless we force him to spend money," Patricia observed.

"When you promised him we'd find a brilliant submissive, Marguerite, did you mean an extremely smart or an extremely servile one?" asked Laura.

"Either," replied the redhead gaily.

"You know he's staying in the village tonight," said Patricia.

"He might appreciate some company for dinner," Marguerite returned, then both she and Patricia looked at Laura.

"He liked you," said Patricia.

"Yes, he liked you best," agreed Marguerite.

"No, he didn't," Laura disagreed.

"He told us he wanted us to find him someone just like you," said Patricia.

"You must be hallucinating. I almost lost him during the interview because I asked some questions that revealed what a ball buster he really is," Laura declared.

"Excuse me," said Patricia, "but are we talking about the same gentleman?"

"The man was completely stuck on himself," said Laura.

"He was somewhat full of himself, at first, I'll grant you," said Marguerite, "but I observed the attitude drop as the interview progressed. He seemed a good deal more animated and real towards the end."

"Yes, especially when he was discussing his examining room," said Patricia. "I'd love to see it."

"What you saw was him getting more and more flustered at me

between the cuts," Laura admitted.

"He's cute," said Patricia.

"I don't want to play with him," said Laura.

"Just have dinner with him and let him spank you," said Patricia.

"No!" said Laura heatedly.

"Don't you want to keep our richest client happy?" Patricia pressed her friend. "After all, he came all the way to Random Point to meet us."

"If you like him so much, you go play with him," Laura advised.

"But he preferred you."

"Patricia, when we started this business nothing was said about playing with the clients," Laura reasoned, "and furthermore, doesn't that defeat the whole purpose of what we are trying to do?"

"Ordinarily I wouldn't suggest it, but he's so handsome and rich. How could you resist?" Patricia continued to tease Laura. Then Laura arose with a dangerous look and went for the phone to dial a number she had memorized.

"Hello, Connie? Would you please ring Dr. Honeywell's suite?" said Laura to the Innkeeper of the Bone and Feather. "You brought this on yourself," said Laura softly to Patricia, with her hand over the receiver. "Oh, Dr. Honeywell? This is Laura Random. How are you? May I tell you why I'm calling? Thank you! You see, my partner Patricia Fairservis only just found out you were going to be in town tonight and although she's too shy to ask you yourself, I know for a fact that she would love to have dinner with you.... You will? Eight o'clock? She'll be there."

"I wish you hadn't done that!" cried Patricia as soon as the mischievous brunette put down the phone.

"What's the matter? You were willing to sacrifice me. Since you seem to like him so much, you can suffer in my place."

"Well, I don't mind," smiled Patricia, "but how did he sound when you told him?"

"Surprised and interested."

"You know Hugo would flip if he thought I was playing with the clients for free," Laura said, as she and Marguerite drove back down to the village.

"I understand. Fortunately, your first temptation was resistible," murmured Marguerite.

"Well? Aren't you in the same position with Malcolm?"

"Oh, far worse. We're newlyweds, after all."

"So, we'll just let Patricia handle the social end of things for a while, huh?"

"Until we decide otherwise," Marguerite stipulated.

The next day Laura sent a copy of Julian's tape to Teresa Clifford, a young woman of distinction and numerous connections in the West Coast scene. Laura asked Teresa to recommend a possible playmate for Dr. Honeywell if she could.

When Teresa viewed the tape she was impressed. Bestowing this magnetic male on a friend in the scene would be a favor indeed.

The tape arrived at Zoe Miller's office on a Friday morning but she didn't insert it into her VCR until late afternoon. The young editor sat behind her desk and her best friend, Carlos, the gay office manager sat on the edge and lit both their cigarettes.

"Listen to this," the slim brunette read Teresa Clifford's note to her, "Dear Zoe, Dr. Honeywell is looking for a girlfriend. When you watch the tape you'll see why I thought of you. His phone number is listed at the end."

"Let's see what he looks like," encouraged Carlos.

As soon as the tape began to roll a blush suffused Zoe's fair face.

"Wow," she breathed at length, "I guess he's a spanking person."

"That's your favorite kind, isn't it, Zoe?" Carlos teased her.

"He's very handsome, isn't he?" she replied, looking hard at the screen.

"A little buttoned-down for my taste, but I suppose girls like that fussy, anal retentive look."

"I like his smile when it happens to come out, but he seems a little pompous, don't you think?"

"He's patriarchal, but that's okay. We like that."

"Should I call him?"

"He's a Beverly Hills doctor. That means he'll have both money and drugs. Of course call him."

"You don't think he looks a little, you know, too good for me?"

"Silly."

"That looks like an expensive suit he has on. Look at me," she drew attention to her jeans and flannel shirt.

"So he'll take you shopping."

"I wonder what he means by sexual servitude." For Zoe had been sent the unedited version of Julian's tape.

"If you don't know, who would?"

"I wonder if..."

"...he's big enough to satisfy your endless needs?" Carlos laughed.

"Shut up."

"Size queen."

"If I am I got it from you. And working here."

"Call him."

Dr. Honeywell was packing his briefcase to leave his office for the day when the phone rang at four p.m. His receptionist said it was a personal call from a Zoe Miller.

"Dr. Honeywell?"

"Yes?"

"My name is Zoe Miller. I'm calling because I received a tape of you in the mail today from my friend Teresa Clifford."

"Teresa Clifford the B&D actress?"

"Yes."

"She had my tape?"

"That's where I got it from."

"H'm."

"It was an interesting tape."

"Did you think so?"

"I'm 27."

"That's a charming age."

"I'm career-oriented."

"I approve of that."

"I'm into spanking and always have been."

"When can we meet?"

"I think I should send you a photo first," said Zoe, regarding her reflection in the mirror across her office.

"You sound very cute. I don't need a photo; let's just meet."

"No, I want to send one."

"Mail it today."

Two days later Zoe's photo arrived. He opened the envelope with excitement, knowing he was about to fall in love. Because of her circumspection, he expected more character than beauty in her face, more softness than sleekness in her body. Therefore he was pleasantly surprised by Zoe Miller, a lean girl with long, black, curly hair, a wide mouth and mischievous eyes. Her preppie clothes and clean scrubbed good looks also pleased Julian. He'd asked The Matchmakers to find him someone like Laura, and this girl might have been her sister. He immediately called Zoe to set up a date for that night.

Zoe prepared for her date in a trance, watching Julian's tape again and again as she tried on and discarded many outfits. She finally decided on a cream linen open-collared dress, which she wore with a beige blazer, penny loafers and anklets. She wore her hair down, with a headband that matched the blazer. When she was dressed, she watched the tape again.

When the bell rang she jumped, turned off the TV and ran to door. The little parlor of her West Hollywood cottage was filled with a type of smoke that did not surprise Julian in the slightest.

Merely shaking his hand made her blush to the eyes as she thought about why he was here and what might happen to her later.

"Julian?"

"Zoe. You're much prettier in person than in your photo. And I loved your photo."

Zoe looked embarrassed and stammered out something about a drink.

"Sure," he said, "what have you got?"

"Whatever you like."

"Vodka tonic?"

"I can manage that," she said, going to the freezer for the vodka. Her hand trembled as she prepared the drink.

"I can tell you've been up to something in here, young lady," he said when she came back.

"You did say on your tape that you had no objection to recreational drugs."

"I'm a doctor; I love recreational drugs."

"Really? Do you want some?"

"I'll just drink this for now. What did you do, though, pour half a pint into this glass?" he winced at the strength of the drink she had handed him.

"Want me to re-do it?"

"I don't mind drinking it, but you'll have to drive."

Zoe took the drink back from him and weakened it, deeply respectful of the Mercedes in the driveway. Then they sat across from each other in the cozy, book filled room.

"Smoke some more if it will relax you, Zoe."

Zoe felt abashed that her state of nervous excitement was so obvious yet thrilled by the novelty of the entire situation.

"So tell me, Zoe, what do you do?"

"I'm a writer," she replied.

"Really? What kind of a writer?"

"I'm an in-house editor for one the largest producer of adult magazines in the country."

"Adult magazines?"

"Hardcore, actually.

"You mean like John Holmes stuff?"

"He's dead, but yes."

"A nice girl like you?"

Zoe smiled. "This week I worked on Ass Masters 2, Girls Who Love Big Cocks, Blondes Have More Cum and Fuck Lickers."

"Fuck Lickers?"

"Don't ask."

"Zoe, what do you really do?" he asked, spotting her college yearbook on her bookshelf. "You don't expect me to believe a Sarah Lawrence girl would be writing porno."

"You doubt I write fuck magazines?" She immediately threw open a cedar hope chest filled to the brim with scores of magazines, which she brought out by the handful and spread across the wooden floor.

"These are all magazines I've written this year." She fanned out numerous issues of Girls Who Take It Up The Ass and The Best of Cum. He grabbed one and scrutinized it, looking over the top at Zoe.

"This text has a charm and acuity that doesn't match the pictures."

"You're probably the only one who ever noticed."

"Doesn't it get to you, writing this stuff?"

"It pays the bills."

"I do want to hear all about it, but I'm even more eager to hear what you thought about the tape Teresa sent you."

"I wondered how you had it made."

"Oh, there's a company out in Massachusetts that's dedicated itself to putting spanking people together, and I decided to see what it could do for me."

"Just spanking people?"

"Apparently."

"How wonderful. I had no idea anything like that existed. And I used to live in Boston."

"I take it that your boyfriend doesn't spank you?"

"No, sir, he does not."

"And what does he do?"

"He works in an ad agency."

"Does he know you're seeing me tonight?"

"Yes. I told him it was something I had to do."

"So you're counting on this being an experiment only?"

"I don't know."

"Is that what you're wearing tonight?" he changed lanes abruptly.

"Isn't it okay?" she pinkened a shade as his eyes came to rest on her anklets and smooth, bare calves.

"It reminds me of a prep school uniform."

"Is that not a good thing?"

"Heels and hose would have been more appropriate," he commented without smiling. Her blush deepened as she tried to determine whether she was being teased or rated. "Do you see yourself as a school girl, Zoe?"

"I just thought since you're into it..."

"Yes?"

"It seemed appropriate to me."

"Perhaps for lunch and a museum tour, but not a dinner date."

"Oh."

"Come over here, Zoe," he told her, patting the sofa beside him. She didn't hesitate to join him. "Have you ever had a spanking?"

"Yes, but not often," she replied, her face suffused with color.

He took her by the wrist and pulled her across his lap. Properly positioning her was the work of a moment. "Oh!" she breathed, not unhappily, as he fastened one hand to her waist and smoothed down her skirt.

Smack! His hand came down on her right cheek. Smack! Now he struck the left. The smacks had a full, round, voluptuous feel through her panties and skirt. Alternating cheeks he spanked her firmly ten times. She caught her breath and whimpered every time his palm connected with her upturned, skirted bottom.

"If you dress like a little girl, you risk being treated like one," he warned her, pulling up her skirt to examine her sheer, beige underpinnings. Now he warmed her through her panties, smacking her soundly many times, until the pinkness began to glow through the nylon that encased her shapely, oval bottom.

Meanwhile, Zoe was experiencing a form of arousal she could only define as the sexiest in the world. Compared with this rarified sensation, the pleasures of standard intercourse were but shadows of delight. Certainly it stung and she felt warmth, but the flutters of excitement overwhelmed those of sharp pain to fill her with a dizzying joy.

She knew that this wouldn't have happened with just anyone spanking her. His good looks, pleasant manners and serious demeanor reduced the length of their courtship to minutes. Or rather, hours, if one counted the time she had spent watching the tape.

When Julian pulled her panties down she almost climaxed. Because he was a doctor. Examining rooms had figured largely in her fantasies since childhood.

Julian saw that she was sweetly submissive, prepared to lie across his lap for as long as he saw fit to spank her. He knew that although he was smacking her fairly hard, he was scarcely hurting her. She was so receptive to spanking that even the sharpest swats seemed to thrill her. Having played with so many girls at clubs, he had inevitably come across the handful that were truly submissive, and they had all reacted in a similar way.

He spread her thighs and placed his palm against her damp curls. This electrified her to shudders. Julian's middle finger slipped inside her and bathed in her creamy excitement. Zoe squirmed and ground against his thighs. Still holding her firmly by the waist, he pistoned his finger in and out until she almost came. Then he looked at his watch and noticed that it was nearly time for their dinner reservation.

"This will have to be continued later," he told her, pulling free of her tender grip, pulling her panties back up and setting her back on her feet before him. "We have just enough time to get to The Ivy."

Zoe felt as limp as a wet leaf as he placed her in the front seat of his car and got in beside her with a smile.

"What are you thinking, Zoe?" he asked as he set them on a course for Beverly Hills.

"Nothing."

"Don't lie."

"Do you have a girlfriend?"

"Would I have made the tape if I did?"

"So, what kind of girl are you really looking for?"

"Well, the kind without a boyfriend would have been preferable, but you'll do," he smiled fully at her.

"Come on," she demurred.

"Zoe, why do you think Teresa sent you the tape? You fit the description of the kind of girl I'm looking for perfectly."

"I don't know about that," Zoe protested.

"Oh? And why not?"

"Because I'm not really submissive," she declared apologetically.

"No?"

"Well, no," she returned.

"You certainly take a spanking nicely," he informed her.

"You know, you're a lot less intimidating in person than on film," Zoe told him shyly.

"That's because I'm doing my best to put you at ease. But what do you mean when you say you're not submissive? I was giving you a pretty hard spanking just now and you were getting wet."

"Oh, I'm into spanking, but not the other things you mentioned."

"Really? You wouldn't let me tie you up?"

"Maybe my wrists, but I wouldn't let myself be gagged."

"Not even with a clean, white handkerchief, like on Superman?"

"I suppose Lois and Jimmy did get tied up and gagged quite a bit."

"And you wouldn't suffer yourself to be fitted for a custom waist cinch?"

"Weren't corsets the reason Victorian ladies were always having fits of the vapors?"

"But what magnificent figures they achieved."

"And I'm not exactly sure what you meant by the term role playing," Zoe remarked as he gave his car to the valet and led her into the restaurant.

Once they were seated Julian replied.

"Well, an example of role playing would be you coming to my office, as though you sought a medical consultation, and me behaving like the authoritative physician that I am."

"You mean in the way you discussed on your tape?"

"Only if that sort of thing interests you."

"It does," she replied, coloring again.

After dinner Julian took Zoe back to his house, which was a small, Tudor style mansion set well back on Maple Street in Beverly Hills. Zoe was dazzled and intimidated. But after a liqueur and a smoke in the sitting room, she seemed almost ready to play.

Julian told Zoe that she was much too well educated to be a porno writer and suggested that she should be punished for the inertia that had kept her in the same position for over a year. Since Zoe was fairly indifferent to her job, she allowed him to pull her across his lap once more.

Once again, he gave her a good spanking and once again, she responded to it passionately. But the dream of erotic perfection fell apart when he determined to send her to the corner.

Zoe, who had just been put off his lap looked at him and explained,

"I don't want to stand in the corner. It's just not me."

Julian had instructed every girl he had ever spanked at a club to stand in the corner and none had ever argued about it. He suddenly realized that having been paid for their time, they were obliged to obey him, while Zoe had consented to see him only to please herself. He wondered whether all non-professional submissives were as willful as Zoe. Was it possible the club scene had fostered a belief in a kind of woman who didn't exist in the real world?

"Do it to please me," he told her coolly.

"I'd feel silly."

"Don't you feel silly getting a spanking at your age?"

"Oh no! That feels divine."

"So you won't obey me in this one small request?"

"I'd prefer not to," she said stubbornly.

Julian was on the point of taking her back across his knee and spanking her until she agreed to obey him. He could spank her much harder than she liked and force her to comply with his simple request. But, would he ever see her again if he did?

"I'll ask you one more time to obey me and stand in the corner," he said sternly. Zoe hadn't wanted to make him angry, but she shrunk from the indignity of being placed in the corner. Tears pricked the corners of her eyes.

"I don't want to," she decisively refused.

"Very well," he said, cold and offended. "Then perhaps I'd better take you home now."

"Okay," she said shakily, pulling on her blazer and biting on her trembling lower lip. When he saw the effect his sudden harshness had on her, Julian's cock throbbed with excitement. But she had to be taught a lesson for placing her dignity above her dominant's gratification.

Julian hardly spoke as he drove Zoe home. Meanwhile she went over the events of the evening in her mind and still believed that they ought to be making love now.

When they stopped in front of her cottage, she fled the car with a hasty good-bye and a tear in each eye. Julian drove away immediately, frustrated and angry both with her and himself. Meanwhile Zoe locked the door behind her and burst into sobs, feeling terribly punished.

But the next morning she awoke with a fresh point of view and immediately dialed Julian's home number. His machine answered and she identified herself. A moment later, Julian picked up.

"Julian, I just called to thank you for dinner."

"Thank you for joining me," he replied without much warmth.

"And I did want to ask you a question," Zoe added without hesitation.

"Okay."

"Julian, I realize that our evening didn't go quite perfectly, but the very fact that it happened at all was an amazing thing to me, being as I needed so desperately to play."

"I understand," he said, softening a little.

"Well, I wanted to thank you for that. I mean, for making the session so agreeable."

"It was agreeable to me as well," he said, unbending a little more.

"I do wish that we were better suited to each other. But since we're obviously not, I was wondering whether you would mind if I got in contact with the company that shot your video, so that I could make a tape of my own?"

After two seconds of silence Julian laughed. "You little brat," he murmured, though not disrespectfully.

"But, why?" Zoe smiled at her own genius.

"I think we're perfectly suited to each other," he said evenly. "You just need to be taught better manners."

"By you?" she laughed, remembering how rudely he had taken her home.

"When can I see you again?"

"I really don't think –" she began to demur but he interrupted her firmly.

"Never mind that, you've won the round and I acknowledge it."

"But, about the corner time..."

"I'll never mention it again."

"It really hurt my feelings being taken home like that," she declared. "I cried myself to sleep."

"I'll make it up to you," he promised, thinking of a shopping trip.

"I was ready to let you make love to me in any way you liked."

"If I acted like an idiot, it's only because I've been spoiled by well-trained B&D club submissives. Did you really cry yourself to sleep?"

"I hope you don't like that idea."

"I do find it very sexy, but I'm sorry about last night."

Zoe paused a moment before speaking. At least he had said he was sorry at last.

"How did you intend to make it up to me?" she asked casually.

"By indulging you completely the next time we meet."

"In your examining room?" she asked with shy excitement. Julian looked at the receiver with surprise.

"Is that your idea of total indulgence?" he laughed. "I was thinking more in terms of a trip to Christian Dior and a weekend getaway to a five-star inn."

"It would be too early to commit to a weekend," she pointed out sensibly. "And that kind of shopping trip sounds like you'd own my soul afterwards."

"So you want to see my examining room, do you?" Julian was charmed.

"Yes."

"You know what will happen when I get you in there, don't you?"

"No."

"Well, for one thing, you'll have to do a better job of obeying me than you did last night."

"Or else what?"

"Or else I'll spank you a lot harder next time and whip your bottom too."

A moment's silence ensued. Then Zoe said, "I don't mind that."

"You just don't want to stand in the corner."

"Right."

"Anything else I should know?"

"If I think of anything, I'll tell you."

"I'm sure you will."

Zoe got her trip to Christian Dior and the weekend at a Santa

Barbara inn, with the office visit between, beginning on the following Saturday afternoon.

Julian explained that he couldn't take her back to the office and expect complete privacy until after four, so after picking her up at her house, they drove directly to Rodeo Drive and Julian dragged her into three or four stores. Zoe stood speechless as he conferred quickly and authoritatively with sales women about gown sets, corsets, dresses and shoes. Nothing was tried on after she was judged to be a size 4 who looked best in creams and beiges. Charge cards came out and purchases were made.

He then conducted Zoe, who now felt loved, to his office on Roxbury Drive.

They passed through a large, elegant waiting room and into a dignified consultation room, with dark green walls and book-lined shelves.

"Have a seat," said Julian, going behind his large desk and motioning her to the chair before it. "I've got some questions I want to ask you."

Zoe obeyed him while looking around with great interest.

"Any persistent health problems, Miss Miller?" he asked, opening a folder and tagging a chart with her name.

"No. Except for headaches."

"Do you have a headache now?"

"No."

"What do you think causes them?"

"Stress."

"Well, Miss Miller, you probably can't reduce the stress in your life, but giving up cigarettes and reducing your caffeine intake may help. I also recommend a detox session, which I do have time to administer now."

Zoe stared at him wordlessly.

"Do you elect to receive the treatment?" he asked, pushing a piece of paper across the desktop for her signature.

"I do," she agreed shakily, taking up a pen and signing her name at the bottom of the proffered medical form.

"In that case, young lady, you may precede me into the examining room and remove your clothes. I'll join you presently."

Zoe looked at the door but didn't move. "Now?"

"Yes, now."

Julian's examining room was the type that had been designed to impress stylish, young Beverly Hills matrons. Even the fresh, cream cotton robe that had been set out for her behind the dressing screen bore a Fernando Sanchez insignia. This Zoe pulled on over her sheer beige bra and panties, leaving the rest of her clothes folded in a wooden cupboard.

She had a moment or two to wander around the ebony and cherry wood paneled room with its fascinating examining table and chair. Discreetly framed on one wall was a gallery of beautiful female faces, the "after" photos of many of the subjects he had worked on. Julian's specialty was eyes and he did admirable work. Zoe was examining the portraits when he entered.

"Miss Miller, are we going to have problems so soon? Didn't I tell you to get completely undressed?"

"But it was such a pretty dressing gown, I had to try it on."

"Well now you can take it off," he told her sternly, turning his back on her to remove his jacket and wash his hands.

Zoe reluctantly removed the robe and hung it back where she had found it, then shyly came forward in her pretty nylon combination. Julian sighed.

"Undress completely, Miss Miller," he told her, opening a lower cabinet drawer to remove the several pieces of equipment he would need to perform the ritual he had promised. Zoe's eyes widened at the sight of the large, black hot water bag, long hose and thick white nozzle.

She watched him wheel an I.V. stand to the side of the flat, green leather examining table.

"Come over here, Miss Miller," he said, patting the table. Zoe came to him and let him lift her to the table. Reaching around her back he unhooked her bra and freed her small, round, stiff-nippled breasts from its confines. "I'm sorry if it embarrasses you, but the procedure to follow does require full nudity," he explained, cupping one breast in

23

each hand and squeezing them lightly. Zoe whimpered as hot thrills surged through her. "And you promised to obey me," he reminded her, gently easing her onto her back on the table, then rolling her over onto her tummy. "Is this your idea of obedience?" He stroked her upturned bottom through her panties, then spanked her soundly ten times. "I told you to remove every stitch, Miss Miller. It's not an unreasonable request."

Now he hooked his thumbs into the waistband of her briefs and pulled them slowly down to her upper thighs, baring her pinkened bottom. "Keep your tummy flat against the table," he told her, holding her with one hand in the small of her back while he used the other to continue spanking her. Zoe hid her face in her arms and submitted, madly aroused.

"This isn't the only spanking you're getting today, Miss Miller. Wait till you feel how hard I spank you once your little tummy has been filled."

"No!" she murmured, nevertheless arching to his hand and spreading her thighs as much as the binding briefs would allow.

"What did I say about keeping your tummy pressed to the table?" he asked, smacking her a little harder. Zoe subsided again and almost climaxed from the sensation of cool leather pressed under her swollen clit. "Can't you obey the simplest command?"

"I'm sorry," she cried, wriggling so cutely that he paused to place a kiss behind her ear.

"Never mind. Since you're so impatient to show off, we'll proceed immediately," said Julian, pulling her panties off entirely now. "Up on your knees, young lady, but keep your elbows on the table."

When Zoe's bottom was uppermost, Julian separated her knees as far as they would go, leaving her upturned and spread, with her tiny bottom hole completely accessible to his view and touch.

Slipping a palm under her pussy, Julian felt her very wet curls. The next thing he did was to don a pair of gloves, open a tube of KY and spread her cheeks apart to apply it liberally to her anus. Lubricating Zoe made her nearly dizzy.

"Keep your legs apart and don't move until I return," he warned her, spanking her low on her bottom, just above her pussy several times before going away to fill the bag with very warm water.

"Have you ever had an enema, Miss Miller?" he asked, returning and affixing the hot water bottle to the I.V. stand.

"No, sir," she murmured, trembling in every cell as she watched his movements in a mirror opposite the table. Deftly he squeezed the excess air out of the hose and lubricated the long, white nozzle.

"It may feel a bit uncomfortable at first, but you'll get used to it." He pressed the nozzle against her slick anus lightly, pulling her apart as he did so, until the tip eased in. She groaned at the gentle intrusion, humiliated to her soul but in a kind of ecstasy. "You know, Zoe, you're not really here for a detox," he told her firmly. "You're here to be disciplined."

"Oh!" she replied, thrilled and afraid.

"That's why this will be a retention enema," he informed her, inserting the nozzle slowly and deeply into her bottom. "You need to be humbled for your willfulness."

The girl who refused utterly to stand in the corner, submitted unreservedly to the sentence that he had pronounced, feverishly excited by the nozzle penetrating her bottom.

"Ready, Zoe?" he asked. When she murmured her assent, he released the clamp on the hose and began the flow of hot water. It did feel slightly uncomfortable at first, and very warm. She almost cried out in fear of the sensation. But the next moment intensely erotic sensations began to flow through her entire sex. The ticklish hose in her bottom brought her to the edge of orgasm again and again as the warm water filled her. Julian was aroused by her tender passivity.

"You are a stubborn girl, aren't you?" he demanded, placing one hand under her satiny belly. A tremor passed through her at this exquisite touch.

"No, sir!" she assured him, with eyes shut tightly.

"I know a stubborn girl when I meet one," he told her, slipping one finger up into her slippery sex.

"Oh!" she cried in surprise. He played with her for a minute or two then took away his hand. Zoe was once again on the edge of a climax, she, who almost never came!

"Think of it, Zoe, for the first time in your life, you're getting a punishment enema. And from a qualified physician."

Zoe could hardly think of anything else at the moment—except for how handsome Julian looked with his sleeves rolled up. He stopped the flow of the water momentarily, to let her get used to the fullness of her belly and get his fingers wet in her pubic curls. Then he resumed filling her until the bag was empty.

"There," he said, carefully removing the nozzle from her bottom and patting away the stray water droplets with a towel, "now don't move."

Zoe didn't dare move.

Suddenly he was in front of her, calmly opening a medical bag to withdraw a medium sized rubber retention plug.

"See this?"

"Yes."

"This is going in you now," he told her, then went behind her again, spread her bottom and inserted the 5" plug deeply into her rectum. This elicited a charming whimper from Zoe, who again nearly came from the indescribable sensations of pleasure and shame this new intrusion produced.

The next object Julian removed from the bag was a medium-sized rectangular wooden paddle, which he immediately laid against the rubber plug. He then proceeded to lightly paddle the plug into her bottom while cradling her public mound in his hand.

When Zoe began to whimper he pulled back and laid the paddle against her bottom cheeks, spanking her firmly with it. Then he alternately paddled the butt of the plug and the fleshiest portion of her buttocks, until she sobbed with emotion.

"You're a bad girl," he told her firmly and was gratified by the tremor that passed through her at these words. He smacked her hard across both cheeks with the shiny maple paddle. "I'm going to train you to take even more stringent forms of discipline before too long, Zoe," he promised. "If I only had a vibrator here, I'd show you. I'd take you across my knee, full as you are, and keeping the plug in your bottom, I'd insert the vibrator into your pussy as far as it would go, and turn it on while I was spanking you." Smack! The paddle came down hard across both plug and spread cheeks. "I'll do that next time,"

Julian promised, causing Zoe to finally succumb to the most euphoric climax of her life.

For a couple of weeks, Zoe was in heaven. To finally have a lover into spanking and anal humiliation was too much joy. Her work suffered and her straight relationship disintegrated like sugar in water. She was on the brink of being fired for spending half her time writing love letters and erotic fantasies to Julian. Then cold reality hit her in the face.

It was a Friday night and she had driven straight from work to Julian's house intending to await his arrival. She was passing through the main hall when her eye strayed to the overflow of mail coming through the slot in the wall. She approached the pile of mail and fell to her knees on the floor with a pounding heart. There were several colored and/or scented envelopes, addressed in feminine hands, and a number of other plain white ones, all with the return addresses of women.

It had happened. The thing she had resisted considering, yet feared would separate her from Julian. His ad was out. And sure enough, also in the mail was the very first issue of the Matchmakers club publication. Frenzied with curiosity, Zoe worked open the brown envelope to pull out the thick digest. There, on page 16, in a full-page ad, was Julian's handsome, suited portrait. The ad had been submitted to The Matchmakers before meeting Zoe. And there had been no way to pull the ad in a timely manner. But now it was out for all to see, and witness the response! The first day and already he had a mailbox full of letters.

She sat on the carpet reading over his ad many times. It reiterated much of what had been in the tape, which she hadn't watched again since first meeting him. As Zoe read of how he sought a true submissive for esoteric B&D, she wondered how many of the girls who had responded to his ad fulfilled Julian's requirements better than she. Suppose eight out of ten were eager and willing to stand in the corner, for instance? And three of those were pretty? And one brilliant?

She was still sitting on the floor and staring at the letters when

Julian walked in. She sprung to her feet guiltily, allowing the Matchmakers booklet to fall on the floor. A deep blush suffused her cheeks as he eyed her and the digest.

"Hi," he said, stooping to pick up the mail and the issue.

"Hi."

"What are you doing?"

"Nothing."

"Nothing besides opening my mail?"

"Just the Matchmakers book, Julian. I was just so curious to see it," she explained, with a pounding heart.

He frowned at her a moment then said, "Come with me."

Julian led her into his study and motioned for her to sit down in the chair opposite his massive desk. After momentarily scrutinizing her fair face he directed his attention to the booklet and began to leaf through it.

"Your ad came out well," she commented shakily. "You look handsome." He merely raised his eyebrows at her then continued to read. After a few minutes of uncomfortable silence he put down the booklet and turned his attention to the many letters. He leafed through them, shuffled them, then stacked them neatly in a pile. There were ten replies in all. Julian looked at Zoe.

"I should punish you severely for opening my mail," he speculated. She flashed him one resentful pout then jumped to her feet.

"I'd better go now. I'm sure you want to be alone to read your mail."

"You'll go when I tell you to go," he snapped, causing her to subside in the chair.

"You certainly got a lot of responses," she commented boldly.

"A surprising amount," he agreed, amused by her jealousy.

"I guess you won't be needing me anymore," she blurted out, with a catch in her voice. Then she sprung up again and made for the door.

"Zoe, where do you think you're going?"

"I'm sorry, I can't stay now. I'm too upset!" She ran out of the room, but he followed her and brought her back by the hand.

"Sit down," he pushed her towards the tufted leather sofa. "You're going to read the letters to me." By now Julian had become very attached to Zoe and could not imagine anyone more desirable presenting herself to him. Just that morning he had sent The Matchmakers a handsome check for the introduction and had instructed them to pull his ad from the publication.

However, the prospect of all these adventurous new women offering themselves to him could not fail to intrigue the doctor, and he knew that his nature would compel him to follow up on any of the letters that seemed interesting.

Zoe accepted a letter opener and slit the first envelope. It contained a single sheet of pink paper, inscribed in a round, childish hand. There was no photo and the contents of the letter were too bland to frighten her. It was simply a letter from a 30-year-old computer consultant into spanking. She seemed inexperienced, compliant, awed by Julian's photo but not particularly bright. Julian took the letter and told her to open the next one.

The next letter came with a photo depicting a plain, plump young woman in a black bra, panties and garter belt. She was turned with her face to the wall in a dreary apartment and her letter was equally unappealing. She claimed to be into every aspect of B&D, particularly that of sexual servitude.

"I'm not surprised, with that presentation," Zoe snorted, slightly cheered by the contents of the first two letters. Several more letters from sincere but ordinary young women followed, generally accompanied by fuzzy snap shots. Some of the letters were surprisingly graphic, others timid and paranoid. None so far bore the stamp of originality. They flirted heavy-handedly. Not one was clever.

But the last letter was different. It came in an 8" x 10" envelope that also disgorged a glossy black and white still. Zoe's heart contracted with pain and fear when she beheld a small waisted, stringently corseted blonde, who appeared to be of legal age, but only barely, with her long, straight hair down her back and a provocative expression in her wide, light eyes. She perched on the edge of a chair, her wrists apparently bound behind her back, her ample, surgically enhanced bosom thrust up and out and her bare bottom elegantly displayed as she sat turned three quarters from the camera lens.

Zoe handed Julian the photo with a shaky hand and lit a cigarette before reading the letter aloud.

"*Dear Doctor,*" she began, glancing up to watch Julian's reaction to the beautiful, professionally photographed portrait. "*I'm a single female, 23, 5'6", 120 lbs., with measurements of 34D, 24", 35". I graduated from U.C.L.A. last year with a degree in Communications. I'm currently employed as a freelance model. My photo spreads have appeared in Penthouse and Skin Two. I've felt myself to be submissive ever since reading The Story of O while still in high school, but it's only recently that I've begun to explore this facet of my character.*

I don't have a boyfriend at the moment because none of the men I know are the slightest bit dominant, although my recent discovery of OOTC has allowed me to play a bit at parties.

I was attracted to your ad because I'm quite desirous of meeting a handsome, experienced, generous, older man to guide me on my odyssey in the scene.

I love spanking, whipping, caning, bondage, anal erotica, oral servitude, immobilization and sensory deprivation, and am extremely interested in having my nipples as well as my labia pierced.

I live in West L.A. and would be free to get together any evening. If interested, please give me a call at the number below.

> *Waiting for your command,*
> *Gloria Lindstrom.*"

"Wow," said Zoe. "She seems just perfect for you, Julian."

"Think so?"

"She's got everything you're looking for and more."

"Except for the fact that she's not my type," he pointed out.

"In what way is Gloria not your type?"

"She's too young. What could we possibly have to talk about?"

"With that body why would you even need to talk?"

Julian merely smiled and said, "I'm also pretty sure she's a pro."

"Because she wants a generous lover?"

"That and her eagerness to please."

"But that comes with the territory, doesn't it?"

"In your case it certainly doesn't."

"And you're so generous anyway, what does it matter if she is a pro?"

"I've dated models before. They're boring."

"How can you say that, Julian? This girl is "Beauty" incarnate. Everything about her screams perfect submissive."

"Maybe I prefer my imperfect submissive."

"You mean me?"

"Who else?"

"But you're going to call her, aren't you?"

"I'll probably call her once."

"Right," said Zoe, the color rushing to her face.

"One date should satisfy both my curiosity and hers."

"What's OOTC?"

"Out of the Closet. That's the local B&D support group."

"I never heard of it."

"I'll give you their newsletter."

"I expect you'll be getting replies every day from now on."

"Mmmm."

Zoe took up the Matchmakers publication and began to read the ads from local men.

Two weeks later Zoe arranged to attend her first OOTC party with Teresa Clifford. It was held in a large meeting hall on Ivar Street in Hollywood that at ten o'clock was packed with a couple of hundred B&D enthusiasts. Zoe was clad in a black leather halter dress and 4" pumps bought for her by Julian.

As soon as Zoe and Teresa entered the first crowded room, submissive males who begged them to whip or spank them or let them worship their feet surrounded them. Zoe declined all offers, not feeling the slightest bit dominant in spite of her outfit. Teresa took a seat and allowed a slave to adore her 5" heeled, thigh-high boots. Zoe left her to wander around the room and stare in wonder at the floggings, wax drippings and stringent bondage positions being tried out on willing submissives.

Many of the players were situated on the wrong side of 40, with scary physiques. The scenes in which they were participating did not arouse Zoe, but she appreciated the whole on a Diane Arbus level and found herself amused for a half hour before going to seek out Teresa again. But as she made her way through the room to find her friend she was struck by the entrance of Julian Honeywell with Gloria Lindstrom in tow.

Gloria was every bit as striking as her photograph and was in fact clad in the same custom corset she had worn while posing for it. Her heels were even higher than Zoe's and both her bosom and bottom were completely exposed. She seemed in a trance as Julian led her through the room by a leash attached to a studded dog collar that encircled her throat. Her eyes never left the ground before her and her posture was all compliance.

Zoe darted behind a pillar before they passed and watched them from this vantage point. The view of Gloria from the rear was nothing if not daunting, with her long legs and smooth round cheeks so exquisitely set off by the hip length corset.

Zoe's heart pounded as she watched her beautiful rival follow her lover through the room. They stopped at a raised platform that Julian mounted, pulling Gloria behind him. Upon this platform stood a wooden X-frame to which leather cuffs had been attached. Julian put Gloria's wrists and ankles into the cuffs, spreading her legs well apart as he did. Then he took up a long, multi-thonged, leather flogger and began to lightly feather her bottom, gradually increasing his tempo and the force with which he was wielding the whip.

Zoe watched in distraught fascination as the whipping progressed, able to observe Gloria's face each time the lashes struck. The model appeared in a reverie as people gathered to watch. The blonde girl looked very submissive indeed, with a soft, babyish quality to her skin and even a slight suggestion of voluptuousness around the tummy, buttocks and thighs that hadn't appeared in the photo she'd sent. Even so, it was difficult to ascertain whether Julian was having a good time.

"What a handsome man," Teresa remarked to Zoe when she found her observing the pair on the platform. "He seems somehow familiar."

"I'm not surprised. That's the one who's tape you sent me. Remember?"

"Oh yes! The Beverly Hills doctor. Whatever happened with you two?"

"We've been seeing each other."

"So what's he doing here with the princess?"

"You know her?"

"Gloria? Sure, she's pretty much this year's sub."

"Is she a pro?"

"Oh, I should think so."

"She answered his Matchmakers ad."

"Really? She must be looking for a master."

"Have you ever talked to her?"

"We've worked together on a couple of video shoots. She's adorable but not terribly bright. She can take plenty of whipping though. Great pain tolerance. Loves to be gagged. Into suspension bondage and ripe for piercing."

"I'm sure I've lost him."

"Think so?"

"How can I compete against that sort of submissiveness? I won't even let him stand me in the corner."

"Admirable," Teresa smiled. "Maybe you're a dominant at heart."

"I wish I could talk to her alone. See what she's like," said Zoe.

"Wait till she hits the ladies room and follow her in."

Zoe waited a half hour before spotting Gloria enter the restroom then took Teresa's suggestion. While the younger girl was reapplying color to her full lips, Zoe came in and began to brush her hair.

"Excuse me," said Zoe, making eye contact in the mirror, "but weren't you doing that sexy whipping scene with the handsome man?"

Responding as expected to the flattering tone of Zoe's query, Gloria began to sing the praises of her escort and herself.

Zoe was duly informed of Dr. Honeywell's profession, his residence, his income, stock portfolio and penis size. She was told of Julian's complete infatuation for Gloria, what he had promised to do for her, what presents he had already given her and more.

"He says he's never met anyone like me," Gloria bragged. "He compared me to "Beauty," as in Anne Rice's Sleeping Beauty books."

"Did he?" Zoe smiled.

"Oh yes. Of course, my nose is slightly different than "Beauty's" and that does bother me. But fortunately Julian specializes in that kind of surgery. He says I can have any kind of nose I like!"

"Wow," marveled Zoe, "that must be a five thousand dollar value, at least!"

"God yes!" agreed Gloria guilelessly.

"So what's he like to play with?"

"Perfectly charming."

"What's he into?"

"Oh, spanking, humiliation, breast punishment, hot wax, dildoing, oral sex, anal sex."

"I hope he practices safe sex!" said Zoe in spite of herself, for she always did.

"Well, he is a doctor," Gloria informed her. "But sometimes I think he's too cautious."

"How do you meet someone like that? Not at a place like this, I'm sure."

"Oh no! But there's this wonderful organization back East that just exists to get submissive girls lovers. Here, I even have a card." Gloria withdrew a Matchmakers, Inc. card from her tiny purse and handed it to Zoe. "Subscribe to their publication and you'll meet the most upscale dominants in the country."

"Can this be true?"

"All I know is, I'm sleeping on Ralph Lauren sheets tonight," Gloria blithely confessed before drifting out the door. "Good luck!"

Zoe made her way through the crowded rooms in a heartbroken daze clutching the Matchmakers card in her hand. On her way towards the door as she passed through the bar she was suddenly confronted by Julian.

"Zoe! I had no idea you'd be here!" Julian protested, distressed.

"It's okay, I'm just leaving."

"How long have you been here?"

"Long enough to have met Gloria. I was sure you two were perfect for each other and I was right. Excuse me." Zoe pushed passed him, a lump in her throat.

"Wait a minute," he grabbed her wrist and pulled her back. Without asking her leave, he unceremoniously lifted her to a bar stool and capturing her hands in his, made her look at him. "Just what did Gloria tell you?"

"Only that you're about to make her your mistress."

"Oh, Zoe, that's not true!"

"You're madly in love with her. She's your own little Beauty, or she will be once you've chiseled her nose."

"She does want a nose job," Julian admitted, "but I keep telling her I only do eyes. Don't you see, Zoe? She's grossly exaggerating everything I've said to her."

"So you didn't take her shopping on Rodeo Drive just like you did me?"

"I did take her shopping, but it was more or less in payment for our one and only other date."

"Just the way you paid me?" Zoe asked peevishly.

"Not at all. I paid a hell of a lot more for the privilege of meeting you, young lady."

"What's that supposed to mean?"

"You know I met you though a private introduction."

"I don't understand."

"It's a service The Matchmakers provide. I told them to go shopping for me and they found you."

"Whereas Gloria was connected enough to find you herself!"

"She is a bit of a prodigy when it comes to the scene," Julian admitted.

"You said you only planned to see her once," Zoe pointed out.

"Well, I was curious about these OOTC parties and you can't go to one unless you're a member or a member takes you as a guest."

"I see. Excuse me," said Zoe, jumping off the stool and trying to exit the room. Julian followed her out to the street where she leaned against the old brick wall as hot tears clouded her eyes.

"Zoe, come back inside. This neighborhood isn't safe," he insisted.

"You go back inside. Your submissive is awaiting your command."

"I'm not leaving you out here by yourself."

"Oh, all right!" Zoe replied and marched back inside.

Almost immediately they encountered Gloria who had been searching the rooms for her escort.

"Oh master! There's a man who wants to ask your permission to play with me." Gloria confessed with some excitement.

"Tell him yes," Julian encouraged her, anxious to continue his conversation with Zoe.

"Thank you, master!" Gloria cried and disappeared into the other room to submit to a rope enthusiast's art.

"You see how meaningless this is?" Julian demanded of Zoe.

"All I see is that you've found exactly the kind of girl you specified in your ad and on your tape," Zoe replied over folded arms. Taking her expression of resentment for dominant scorn, a passing foot slave fell on his knees before her and began to kiss the tips of her pumps.

"What are you doing?" Zoe nudged him away with her knee. "Did I tell you that you could do that?" The foot slave meekly bowed his head, got up and melted back into the crowd.

"You're so cute," said Julian fondly, caressing her smooth cheek. Zoe pushed his hand away with the same disdain she had shown the slave.

"She's sleeping on Ralph Lauren sheets tonight!" were Zoe's last words to Julian before she abandoned him entirely to rejoin Teresa Clifford.

Julian scowled with vexation. Zoe's combativeness was annoying. Did she think she could turn on her heel and walk away from him like that?

Gloria's scene with the rope man lasted a half hour, during which time Julian moodily circled the rooms, keeping his eye on Zoe all the while. Now she remained exclusively by the side of the glamorous Teresa, who introduced her to local players.

Finally Julian overheard Zoe consenting to be spanked, then and there, by a young man who was one of the few beside himself not dressed in fetish attire. Unable to resist joining the semi-circle of voyeurs who instantly formed to watch the new girl being spanked, Julian found himself standing close enough to hear the interchange between the stranger and Zoe as it progressed.

First the man clumsily pulled up the tight, expensive, leather dress with Zoe's anxious cooperation, to expose her pantied, garter-belted bottom. Julian recognized the expensive French combination he had bought her just the other day at Barney's, and a puff of indignation swelled his chest.

Being neither a polished nor experienced spanker, the young man brought his hand down with the full force of his arm. Zoe cried, "Hey!" and twisted on his lap, trying to slide off. The young man tightened his grip on her waist and walloped her hard three more times, which caused her to violently kick and loudly protest. Julian was momentarily amused.

"Mercy!" Zoe cried angrily.

The young man ignored her plea and raised his arm high above his head to whack her squirming bottom again. But the crude practitioner was never allowed to continue, for Julian caught his wrist.

"The girl has had enough," Julian told him curtly as Zoe seized the opportunity to scramble off his lap.

"Wait a minute, we were doing a scene," Zoe's towheaded assailant protested with some annoyance.

"She said 'mercy' and you ignored her," Julian firmly replied.

"Hey, are you two posers or what? These parties are for serious players," the veteran member pointed out. Zoe, for her part, could not believe that anyone who could hit so hard could also whine like a girl. Meanwhile, she wasn't sure whether to be grateful to Julian for saving her or angry with him for interfering.

"Excuse me," she said to the offended spanker, then she turned to Julian and muttered a reluctant thank you before marching off to find Teresa, rubbing her bottom through the leather dress as she went.

Julian bristled at Zoe's not according his truly knightly behavior the proper recognition and resolved to teach her better manners at the first opportunity. He watched her rejoin the poised Teresa Clifford with a mixture of admiration and irritation.

Then he looked across the room at his compliant little pat of creamery butter, now coming out of a standing rope tie, all blushes and trembling. She was exactly what he thought he wanted and as it turned out, she bored him to death. Not to mention the fact that her vulgar remarks to Zoe had given him a very real dislike of Gloria.

With sudden decision Julian walked up to Zoe. Surprised and with a fluttering heart, Zoe introduced him to Teresa.

"It's a real pleasure to meet you," said Julian. "I've been a fan for years." Teresa bowed her head with a slight smile. "And I should also thank you for the introduction to Zoe," he added.

"You're welcome. I'm happy to see that it worked out so well," murmured Teresa, excusing herself almost immediately to meet a friend across the room. For Julian was far too attractive for Teresa to risk gazing into the eyes of for more than a moment. Zoe attempted to follow her friend but Julian grabbed her hand before she could get away, the touch electrifying them both.

"Just a minute, young lady. I want to talk to you."

"Yes?"

"Were you going straight home from here?"

"...Yes."

"Good. Because I'll be stopping by around midnight."

"What about Gloria?"

"I'm taking her home now."

"But, aren't you spending the night together?"

"Just be home by midnight," he told her.

"I will be," she replied, with surprising meekness.

Julian made her wait until twelve -thirty before arriving at her door and strolling into her sitting room. Zoe had changed into the taupe silk gown and wrapper set that had been another present from Julian. Outwardly calm, her heart was pounding as she took his jacket from him and put it away.

"Make me a drink," he ordered coolly, "and try to get the proportions right this time." He removed his tie, unbuttoned his collar and rolled up his sleeves. In due time Zoe brought him a carefully prepared vodka tonic, which he took from her and drained in a couple of gulps, causing her eyes to widen. Suddenly flooded with peppery warmth he almost smiled at Zoe's look of consternation. "Good thing you got that right, at least," he tossed off in her direction, unbuttoning another shirt button.

"I'm surprised to see you here tonight," she admitted. "I've never known a man to change his plans before."

"Well, I felt your licking couldn't wait until tomorrow," he explained.

"But what did I do?"

"First of all, you lied to me about what you were doing tonight," he remembered triumphantly.

"I did?"

"Remember I called you yesterday and asked you about your plans for the weekend? You said you were busy Friday night and mentioned something about female bonding. But you never once mentioned that you'd be turning up at the OOTC party. Why not?"

"Because it was a last minute decision, I guess," Zoe hastily explained, knowing full well she had kept her intentions a secret for no reason other than a love of subterfuge.

"Had I known you were going to be there I never would have come with Gloria."

"Is that true?"

"Of course."

"Are you going to see her again?"

"No."

"Because of me?"

"Because of you."

"Oh!"

"You know, Zoe, we really have to discuss this attitude of yours."

"I don't have any attitude."

"Not now, maybe, but you had plenty at the party."

"Did I do something you didn't like?"

"Several things. You let that idiot spank you. You were patently ungrateful when I stopped him from beating you black and blue. You were rude and impertinent when I tried to speak to you. You kept running away from me. And I think that at one point you even stamped your foot."

"I did all of that?"

"I see you're not taking me seriously," he said, stalking her, grabbing her by the elbow and pulling her over to a perfect, armless slipper chair she'd set to one side of the hearth. She pulled back a bit when he tried to take her over his knee but offered little real resistance when he proved determined to pull her over.

He didn't start immediately, but instead increased her tension by positioning her and slowly pushing up both her wrapper and gown to reveal her bare, oval bottom cheeks.

"That idiot marked you," Julian reported, examining the several plum-colored bruises that the player at the party had left on her otherwise flawless bottom. "Why did you ever consent to play with him?" Julian stroked her.

"I was bored."

"Well I can't very well spank you when you're already marked," Julian observed, without releasing her. "I guess I could humiliate you instead." In so saying he divided her cheeks with his fingers.

"But why?"

"To punish you for the insufferably independent attitude you've been displaying all night."

"I'm sorry I'm not as submissive as your Gloria!"

"No you're not," he told her and slapped her hard once on each cheek. "Come to think of it, maybe I should spank you anyway, marks or not." And so saying, he rained a dozen smacks down on her bottom. "You will speak to me in a manner that is civil and polite," he told her, firmly continuing. Again and again he smacked her upturned bottom, until the deep pink coloration left by his hand nearly overwhelmed the earlier marks left by the unskilled spanker at the party. At length this began to really sting and Zoe started to whimper, wriggling on his lap to escape his hand.

Looking around for something thin, hard and smooth to insert into her bottom, Julian espied a white stoneware mortar and pestle on a shelf close at hand. Reaching out he grabbed the smooth ceramic tool that was the perfect shape and size to invade a lady's snuggest portal.

First he got it slippery inside her creamy slit, then he spread her cheeks and inserted it into her anus about four inches, leaving only the rounded knob protruding. Zoe lay quite still as he plunged it in and adjusted the angle of insertion.

"Too bad I don't have any of my enema equipment here," he lamented, patting the dildo in deeper, "then I could be sure of administering an effective punishment to the most impertinent girlfriend I've ever had!" he said with pretended exasperation. "But at least I can spank you," he promised and then began to do just that.

The hard smacks made her pitch and thrash across his lap and the porcelain rod popped out. "Now look what you've done," he scolded. "Didn't I tell you to lie still?" Julian spread her cheeks and held them apart. "Every time you let it slip out you're going to be spanked on the offending area," he warned, slapping her sharply across her spread bottom crack six times. Then he re-lubricated her from her own fragrant and copious juices and reinserted the pestle into her bottom.

Once she was filled he continued the spanking, holding her firmly against his lap by the waist and placing every third smack on the plug. In a minute she was overwhelmed by a rippling climax that soaked his trouser leg with her essence and left her limp. He lifted her off his lap and pointed to her bedroom, sending her off with a smack. She went slowly, looking back at him in a daze.

"Go to bed, you bad girl," he told her, turning off the lights. It was a warm night and he walked into her back garden to smell the lilacs. By the time he joined her in the bedroom she had fallen fast asleep.

Chapter Two

How Cute Is That?

Even though he had been teaching at Hollywood High for twelve years, and had been robbed so often that he now held a gun permit, David Lawrence had not lost his optimism. He was an amiable, youthful thirty-seven, amusing and well liked by both his students and associates, especially the female ones.

Living in the Bladerunner world of modern Los Angeles, he accepted his grim wages, the fact that his marriage had failed and the continuous dangers of his thankless profession without repining. Blessed by nature with wit, remarkably good looks, a cheerful disposition and a propensity for indulging his senses, David found ways to enjoy himself every day.

Meeting women was not a problem, but finding a girl who shared his interest in spanking was. It wasn't enough just to find a woman who would take a spanking. What he really craved was a female counterpart, a fabulous fetishist, who thought about spanking as much as he did.

"It wouldn't have to be someone like Babydoll," he mused, looking out his classroom window, three stories above the intersection of Sunset and Highland, where every day at 3:45, for the last week, the most heavenly little blonde with wavy hair to her waist in a halter top and snug knee pants, on rollerblades, flew down Sunset on the south side of the street, urgently transporting a bag of take-out food.

On day five David made it his business to be out on the street at 3:45. Sure enough, Babydoll passed, this time carrying her take-out in a glossy shopping bag with Clark Gable's photograph on the side. She gave David a quick, little smile as she skated past him, and actually said, "How cute are you?" An instant later, she blushed as she realized that she hadn't meant to say that aloud.

Meanwhile, David was bowled over by his first close-up look at Babydoll. First of all, she was a radiantly beautiful young lady, in her early to middle twenties, whose only business on Sunset Boulevard ought to have been in decorating a billboard. She was in fact, astonishingly beautiful as she turned the corner at La Brea and disappeared.

"I must have imagined I heard that," David mused as he strolled to his favorite coffee bar. He chose a window booth and opened a copy of the L.A. Free Press inside of his L.A. Weekly in order to daydream about visiting one of the B&D salons that advertised in the former.

David didn't bother to go up the counter and order because Brooke Neuman began to prepare his regular double cappuccino as soon as he sat down.

Brooke was the brightest student in David's World Literature class. Her single parent was a subsistence-level stand-up comic and Brooke had to maintain several part-time jobs in order to supply herself with an allowance. David had conversed with her many times and found her both original and charming.

Brooke's graceful form, fine complexion and dark, silky hair barely registered on David because he never thought about his students in that way, although he couldn't fail to notice that she was perhaps the only student at Hollywood High who wasn't either radically pierced or in some way tattooed, and whose hair was all one color.

Brooke's boyfriend, a sardonic German boy named Willie Kronenberg, was the only other brilliant student in the class, but David didn't care for Willie's captious personality and wondered what Brooke saw in him besides his good looks and outstanding grade point average.

Sublimely unaware of the magnitude of crush Brooke had on him, David didn't even bother to close the adult newspaper when she brought his coffee over. He couldn't have closed it at that moment if he wanted to, for he had just seen a photograph that riveted him. In the middle of a two-page spread on a well-bred B&D club called The Keep, there was Babydoll! The girl he had seen on the in-line skates just minutes before and had watched from his window for a week, was billed as a submissive and displayed in a leather halter dress, perched naughtily on a bench with a paddle close by. David's heart leapt so high he nearly choked.

Babydoll available for sessions! His Babydoll. Right here in Hollywood. The ad called her Hope and as both a student of language and a dreamer he took note.

"I can't wait until I'm old enough to work in a B&D club," Brooke remarked to her mentor casually. David gave her a look and smiled, used to her cynical humor. "And that one in particular," she added, beginning to shock him. "I've been staring at their ads for two years."

"Why this one?" he returned off-handedly, wondering whether she was as intuitive as she was precocious.

"The mistress of course," said Brooke. "I love the way she never takes her glasses off. I've written her several letters, but she's firm that I can't even come and visit until I'm eighteen."

"Brooke, you astonish me," David nearly gasped at her temerity. Meanwhile, he thought to himself, "That does it, I'm visiting The Keep today!"

Brooke left him to wait on another customer while David smoked and looked out the window. Finally he got up and went to the phone in the back of the cafe and dialed the number of The Keep. The phone was answered on the first ring.

"Hello!" a euphonious female voice replied.

"Hello," he replied, in his own dulcet tones. "I've been looking at your ad in the Free Press and was wondering what was involved in a visit?"

"Well, what exactly are you looking for?"

"A spanking session."

"Giving or receiving?"

"Giving."

"Well, a half hour session is a hundred, an hour one sixty. Today we have Cherry and Hope available for spankings."

"I'd like to see Hope if I may," said David, throbbing with excitement at his perfect luck.

"She's free right now," the young woman said pleasantly.

"Where are you located?"

The mistress of the house gave David a residential street address not four blocks from where he stood. David promised to arrive within fifteen minutes and went to the counter to pay his bill.

Brooke, who had seemed to be busy the whole time he was on the phone, had none the less noted his every expression and attached great significance to the fact that he had left his paper open to the spread on The Keep before making his call. On his way out he scooped up both his newspapers and departed with an urgency she'd not observed before.

Rushing back to the phone she inserted a quarter in the slot and pressed the redial button. The same mellifluous voice answered, causing Brooke to hesitate a moment before replying, "Mistress Hildegarde?"

"Yes." The voice grew even warmer.

"It's me, Brooke Neuman. Remember? The girl who wrote you the letters?"

"Of course I remember, darling. But do you remember that I told you I couldn't even talk to you until you turned eighteen?" Hildegarde sounded only mildly annoyed.

"I'm sorry," Brooke meekly replied and immediately hung up. Then she ran outside to see whether Mr. Lawrence was still on the street. Luck was with Brooke and she spotted her teacher across the street at an ATM. "Wow, he's really doing it!" she said to herself, racing back inside to tell her boss, Oscar, that she needed an hour to take care of an errand. Then grabbing her camcorder, which she never went anywhere important without, she ran out the door.

Mr. Lawrence had just begun to walk briskly up Sunset. Brooke followed at a distance, filming kids on the street as she went. She had decided to be a filmmaker at age 11 and since then had devoted every leisure moment to watching films, shooting footage and writing scripts.

Mr. Lawrence was easily tracked to the quiet, shabby-genteel side street on which the white wooden house that lodged The Keep was situated. She was even able to video Mr. Lawrence knocking on the door and being given admittance by a gloriously beautiful blonde.

45

In the office of the club, the tobacco-marinated bouncer Rusty watched the closed circuit television monitors that pictured the street with mounting unease. As soon as Mistress Hildegarde came out of session he intended to make her aware of the girl who was taping everyone going in and out of the club.

Meanwhile, David had been taken by Hope up to the blue dungeon.

Since returning to the club and being told that a spanking session was on his way, Hope had changed into a gauzy white party dress and put her hair in a ponytail with a blue satin bow. The dress was new and matched to white pumps.

"We can pretend I'm Carol Linley, circa 1959," she said, when he admired her outfit, for her hobby was the history of glamour and she enjoyed identifying with various periods and looks.

"What's that?" he asked, regarding a form on a clipboard she was preparing to fill out.

"Just your membership application," she explained, handing it to him. "We'll just need you to write your name and address in the blank spaces there."

"Must I? I'm a high school teacher and I'd really rather not."

"You can make up a name, you know. And don't you have a P.O. Box?"

"As a matter of fact, I do."

"I'm sure!" Hope laughed, then observed cleverly, "How else could you receive naughty things through the mail?" Then she looked at him closely. "Do I know you?"

"I work in the neighborhood. Perhaps we've eaten in the same restaurants," he ventured, delighted that she remembered him from their brief eye contact on the street earlier.

"If I'd had teachers as handsome as you I never would have dropped out of college," she confided flirtatiously.

"Dropped out of college, did you?"

"I suppose you don't approve of that."

"You bet I don't."

"Would you like to give me the allowance now so I can take it downstairs and have them start us?"

"Certainly."

David handed her the money and watched her slip out of the room. While she was gone he noticed that someone had placed a paddle, a hairbrush, a strap and a small flogger on a leather-padded bench. The thought of Hope collecting these items for use on her own (no doubt) flawless bottom was sheer heaven.

But oddly, just before she returned to him, the image of Brooke Neuman flashed into his mind. Why would a quiet, thoughtful girl like Brooke dream of working in a place like this?

He paced the room, examined the equipment, lit a cigarette, then pulled the heavy velvet drapes aside to look out the window. What he saw on the street below caused his heart to lurch painfully. There was Brooke Neuman, on the sidewalk opposite The Keep, with her camcorder on her shoulder, blithely taping as she walked up and down. He let the curtain fall back into place and rushed for the door. Then he forced himself to pause and wait for Hope's return.

When Hope came back with a serene smile on her face he allowed himself one moment to appreciate her loveliness before panicking.

"Come here," he said, pulling back the curtain slightly. "Look out there. Do you see anyone across the street?"

"Yes, there's a girl with a camcorder on her shoulder. God, is she taping our front door?" Hope looked at David in alarm.

"That's my favorite student. She must have followed me over here."

"Does she know what kind of place this is?"

"Does she! She wants to work here."

"Oh! Well, she's certainly gorgeous," Hope breathed sincere admiration. "She'd make a fortune."

"She's only seventeen at the moment."

"Ooops. But why is she taping the house?"

"She tapes everything. She wants to make movies."

"I admire her initiative, but we'd better get her to stop filming, before she alarms everyone in the house," Hope said sensibly. "Do you want to go out there and talk to her?"

"Me? God, no!" David protested. "I could probably lose my job for talking to her under these circumstances."

"Is that really true?"

"I have no idea and I don't think I'll ask."

"I'd better go and explain the situation to Mistress. Just wait here. And don't worry."

After Hope's departure David continued to monitor Brooke out the window. In a moment craggy old Rusty crossed the street to confront Brooke, never taking his cigarette out of his mouth or his hands out of his jeans' pockets. No more than two sentences were exchanged before Brooke quickly marched away. Rusty then ambled back to the house and Hope returned to the dungeon.

"It's all taken care of," she reported sunnily.

"What did that man say to her?" David asked with some concern.

"Just that you need a permit to film on the streets of Hollywood."

"Smart!" David was all admiration for Rusty.

"I hope this hasn't put you off playing."

"Oh, no," he replied candidly, hanging his jacket on a peg. Hope gasped as he turned to see the reflection of his gun and shoulder holster in the mirrored wall opposite.

"I thought you said you were a teacher!" she cried with some alarm. "Are you a vice cop? Was that chick your back up? Is this a bust?"

"Not at all. And do calm down. Honestly, I'm just a high school teacher whose been beaten up enough times that they finally gave me a permit to carry a gun." David showed her the permit, his driver's license and teachers' union card. Hope was still skeptical and looked as though she might burst into tears of frustration, for she had been looking forward to playing with him. "Take these to your Mistress," he said with a sigh, thrusting his I.D.s into her hands. "I'll be here."

Hope disappeared yet again, only to return a few moments later, wreathed in smiles. "Hildegarde says I should ask you some questions to make sure you're on the level."

"Oh? What kind of questions?"

"You say you're into spanking, right?"

"Why, yes."

"Prove it."

"How do you mean, prove it?"

"Tell me some things about spanking that you like." Hope sat beside him on the leather covered bondage bed, stretching out her legs to admire the white grosgrain bows that tied across the insteps of her shoes.

"That would take some time," he smiled.

"You haven't proven anything yet."

"Say, how old are you anyway?" he asked her suddenly.

"How old do you think I am?" she laughed.

"Twenty?"

"Thanks! If you are a cop, you're a gallant one. I'm 25."

"That's a relief anyway."

"Oh? You wouldn't rather be spanking your adorable pet with the camera?"

"I'm not interested in my students."

"If that really was your student, I'm sure she has a giant crush on you."

"That's true, girls do get crushes on me from time to time. But she has more common sense than that."

"Then why follow you here?"

"Oh, we had a conversation in the cafe where she works about an hour ago during which she revealed that she's been dreaming about working at this very club for two years. I was indiscreet about telephoning and she was smart enough to follow me."

"So she's brilliant, beautiful, has a crush on her dominant male teacher, and wants to work in B&D. How cute is that?"

"I think one of the things we're going to discuss if we ever do get to play is this Newspeak you kids talk. You, for example, seem smart enough to form more original expressions."

"Now I know you're a teacher!" Hope declared, with an irrepressible grin. Then she hit the intercom button and told Rusty to call them in a half hour.

Except for the nagging sensation of impending doom that set in every time he allowed himself to ponder the notion of Brooke and what she now knew about him, David felt divinely satisfied by his first trip to The Keep.

Spanking the vivacious yet compliant Hope had surpassed all his expectations of sublime erotic pleasure. The way she ground against his lap, the way her alabaster skin had pinkened under his hand, the delicious little gasps she gave as he stroked her in between smacks, all confirmed his long held theory that some women did really enjoy being paddled.

Hope had been all high spirits and ingenuity. She seemed as interested in him as he was in her and made such incisive comments on his favorite subject that he felt as though he was out on the most agreeable date of his life.

When the session ended she had sat on his lap the right way around and given him a tremendous hug, telling him she hoped that he would visit her often. He vowed he would never visit anyone else and pressed a twenty-dollar tip into her hand, wishing it could be more.

Towards Brooke, David's feelings were a mixture of resentment, distrust and uneasy admiration. He felt in his heart of hearts that Brooke would do nothing to hurt him. Not even if he gave her the spanking she deserved for following him to The Keep and setting everyone's nerves a jangle! But given the current climate, he wondered if instead he ought to consult a lawyer before even talking to his student again.

Brooke suffered torments all weekend, wondering whether the walking tobacco stick that had seen her outside The Keep with her camera had informed Mr. Lawrence of her presence there. World Lit was her Monday second period class and the moment he walked in and slammed his briefcase down on the desk she no longer had to wonder.

Normally, Brooke was the first person her instructor smiled at. Today he never glanced her way unless he had to. Of course he had to eventually, because she always raised her hand. Even today, when she wanted very badly not to, pride forced her to do so. They were reading Madame Bovary and she was full of opinions on it.

Willie, who sat directly behind Brooke and noticed everything that pertained to that young lady, marked a difference in their teacher's attitude toward his girlfriend that puzzled the observant boy.

As they left class he demanded an explanation in his usual overbearing style. "How come Mr. Lawrence was ignoring you today?"

"Mr. Lawrence called on me several times," Brooke pointed out, unwilling to be roused from her bittersweet meditations on her idol by her tiresome contemporary.

"Yes, but he didn't commend your responses with his usual enthusiasm. In short, he seemed much less than charmed with you today. What's going on?"

"I don't know. Maybe he's gone off me."

"Aren't you concerned?"

"Why should I be concerned?"

"Weren't you counting on him for your college references?"

"I'm sure he'll give me the references I deserve."

"You know more than you're letting on," Willie accused. But the commencement of their third period American History class cut short the conversation.

Brooke had been going out with Willie since their sophomore year. He was her first lover and she his. Early on she had confessed her spanking fetish. Being a German male, naturally dominant and sexually playful, Willie had given Brooke a spanking on their first date.

They had driven up to the restaurant Yamashiro, which sat atop a Hollywood hill. Brooke had attempted to order wine with dinner, though she only just turned 16. Willie told her, "Behave, or I'll spank you," in front of the waiter.

"They weren't going to proof us," Brooke protested, for it was her birthday and this was her first real restaurant date.

"You need a spanking anyway," Willie told her firmly, causing Brooke to fall instantly in love.

After dinner, while they were waiting for the car to be brought up, they leaned over the parapet to view the magnificent city lights stretching below.

"That reminds me," said Willie, locking one arm around her waist, "you needed a spanking." And briskly he brought his hand down on the seat of her skirt six or eight times, letting her up the very instant the valet drove up with the car.

Brooke shuddered with excitement all the way home. Since it was a night when her father was emceeing at The Star Strip until three a.m., she invited Willie in and her first love affair was begun.

As it later turned out, Willie spanked more out of an innate feeling of male superiority than a desire to arouse her, and this was not an attitude that Brooke was prepared to tolerate much beyond graduation.

David now avoided the coffee bar where Brooke worked. He never addressed a remark to her that wasn't relevant to a lesson or walked with her down the hall chatting. In short, an arctic floe separated them until graduation and well beyond.

Of course David wrote outstanding recommendations for Brooke. By early spring she'd received all her acceptances. She might have gone to Yale if she'd chosen to do so. Instead she picked the U.C.L.A. film school and decided to save on expenses by living at home. She had more than one reason for selecting this option.

Towards the end of the school year, when everyone was discussing his or her college plans, David's resolve never to speak to Brooke again began to weaken. Some months had passed since the incident at The Keep and David was virtually positive that Brooke did not intend to expose him. But there was still the problem of her being underage dynamite. He couldn't risk igniting her with so much as a smile. Even on graduation day, David remained remote.

Brooke felt that she was being cruelly punished, but the firmness of her handsome teacher thrilled her.

Meanwhile, David went to visit Hope once a week, whether or not he could afford it. She was an exquisite addiction.

Then, one Friday afternoon in late September, David arrived at The Keep for his usual appointment and was told that Hope had quit!

"She going to do lots and lots of movies," Hildegarde informed the stunned David. "Don't despair, darling, she was determined that I give you and you alone her number," the pretty mistress told him, writing down the number. "She said she couldn't live without her favorite spanker." David's heart contracted at these soothing words.

"I don't suppose you'll ever find another sub of her quality," he mused.

"I wouldn't be too sure," Hildegarde smiled. "I've got a brilliant little college girl coming to me in October, as soon as she turns eighteen."

"You're not talking about my Brooke?" he snapped back at once.

"Is she your Brooke already?" Hildegarde shook her head with disapproval.

"No, certainly not. In fact, I haven't even talked to her since that incident back in March."

"Neither have I, but I feel certain we'll be welcoming her shortly. In fact, if I were you, I wouldn't miss our Halloween party. October 31st is her birthday."

Not even a large earthquake could have kept David away from The Keep on Halloween. He arrived at eight, in a medium grey pinstriped suit, bearing a large bouquet of red and white Autumn roses, which he had cut from the bushes outside his tiny cottage in Laurel Canyon. Hildegarde was gratified but not surprised by the perfect buds. David's funds were limited but his thoughtfulness was not. In the short time she had known him, he had done her many kindnesses, from driving girls home to editing her advertising copy.

Hildegarde was pouring David a glass of wine in the kitchen when Hope arrived, in a black velvet gown and cape. The blonde girl put one arm around David's waist as she held out her wine glass to be filled.

"Darling, I'm so glad you came," said Hildegarde, who was exactly the same age as her ex-employee and had missed her favorite this last month. "Are you going to play?"

"I think I should. Don't you?" Hope grinned at David, for she knew that he rather enjoyed spanking her after she'd already been spanked hard. "Is she here yet?" asked Hope.

"Not yet," Hildegarde replied.

"She probably forgot all about it by now," David stated with conviction.

"Darling, a girl who's been dreaming B&D for years and who lives ten minutes away from me, is not going to forget about it," Hildegarde declared as the bell rang. "Excuse me," she said, kissing Hope's white throat as she exited.

"What are you going to do and say?" Hope demanded, smiling up at him.

"What do you mean?"

"When she comes in?"

"She isn't coming. But if she does, I don't know."

"You've never been at a loss for words with me," Hope teased him.

A glance upward at the kitchen security camera monitor showed them a leggy young brunette in a black PVC slip dress.

"That's her," David breathed. Hope squeezed his hand.

Brooke was conscious only of a blur of faces as Hildegarde ushered her into the main parlor and relocated a gentleman or two so that they might sit down together on a sofa.

"Mistress Hildegarde, I'm the girl who wrote you those letters this summer," Brooke confided, momentarily riveted by the milky perfection of the club owner's bosom, displayed in a midnight blue velvet bustier gown. "I hope it's all right that I came by tonight," Brooke continued, producing her driver's license and passport for inspection.

"I've been expecting you," Hildegarde told her, handing her identification papers back with a smile. "And so has someone else."

"You mean he's here?" Brooke looked around with a sudden thrill and saw David in the doorway. She thought him more striking than ever and felt her face grow warm as his gaze fell upon her lissome body in the shiny cocktail dress. He approached her with a smile too faint to please her and she wondered whether David was still angry with her for taping him going into the club the previous spring.

"Hello, Brooke. How are you?"

"Is that all you can say to me on the occasion of my 18th birthday and my first visit to The Keep?" Brooke jumped up and impulsively kissed David on the lips. "Please forgive me, Mr. Lawrence, but I've been wanting to do that for several years now," Brooke explained, intoxicated with joy at the coincidence of him being at The Keep on this of all nights.

"Really, Brooke, I would have thought you had more common sense," David scolded, while inwardly aglow. Normally he wasn't attracted to college girls, but Brooke was so sophisticated for her age.

The very fact that the little go-getter didn't seem to need him to accomplish her fantasies raised her to a level of experience he'd not met in women twice her age. Now that it was legal to admire Brooke, he did, though he wasn't about to let her know it.

"Mr. Lawrence, may I ask you a question I've been dying to know the answer to ever since that day I followed you here?"

"You certainly may not," he growled, but then smiled as Hope brought him a glass of wine.

"Hello," said Brooke to Hope.

"Hi. How cute are you?" Hope complimented Brooke.

"Hope, what did I tell you about that mindless incantation?" David demanded with real annoyance.

Hope looked at David with surprise, then, in her usual quick way, realized that David's most intelligent ex-student might not think too well of Val speak. Now Hope blushed deeply as only a natural blonde can, for she was in love with David herself and wanted to be thought well of by him.

"I'd better escape while I can then," Hope smiled with perfect grace at Brooke and avoided David's eyes entirely as she slipped out of the room and ran upstairs to join a friend in a dungeon.

Meanwhile, Brooke had mentally recorded the little scene for all eternity and was moved almost to tears by the pathos of her ravishing rival's humiliation. So this was David's favorite, a heavenly creature as sensitive as she was kind. But David didn't value her, thought Brooke, not nearly as he should.

Brooke was aflame with excitement. Everything was glamorous tonight. To think that the male she worshiped had his own fairy creature to punish and pet was past exotic. She had never seriously thought Mr. Lawrence submissive, but there was always the possibility. Until now, when he had made his attitude so clearly known. Whether in the classroom or the dungeon, Mr. Lawrence remained the instructor.

"Now see here, young lady, you don't seriously mean to come work here?" They sat down in the parlor.

"Why not? It seems to have the nicest clientele," Brooke teased.

"Does your father know you're here?"

"My father knows and approves of everything I do," she returned haughtily, which gave David a start and caused Hildegarde to beam. "You don't think he wants me to graduate college sixty thousand dollars in debt, do you?" the eighteen year old replied sensibly.

"Well, no but—" David stammered.

"My job at the cafe paid seven dollars an hour."

"But a girl like you in a place like this?"

"Don't be disrespectful, Mr. Lawrence," Brooke replied, "after all, Mistress Hildegarde is here."

"Yes, well I'm sure she agrees with me that there are better places for you than in a dungeon," David said with a conviction Hildegarde didn't share.

"David," Hildegarde said, "one of my best girlfriends put herself through law school working for me."

"I never realized you were so stuffy, Mr. Lawrence," Brooke baited him, while looking around the room for the first time at the waiting clients.

"Let's go somewhere and talk," said David impatiently.

"You mean leave now?"

"I do."

"But I just got here."

"Surely you didn't intend to start working tonight?"

"David may have a point, darling," said Hildegarde, cognizant of the hostile looks being tossed in Brooke's direction by several of her other girls. "I've got a full house tonight of both staff and clients and it's unlikely I'll be able to give you a complete tour."

"But I was counting on at least one birthday spanking," said Brooke.

"Is it your birthday?" a plain, conservative looking, fifty year-old male asked with some excitement from a near-by loveseat.

"Yes. I turned eighteen today," Brooke replied.

"God, I'd love to do a session with you," the gentleman vowed. "What's your name?"

"Yes, darling, what is your play name?" Hildegarde ignored David's glower to murmur.

"Do I have to have one?"

"Everyone does."

"I've always liked the name Alison."

"Excellent. Well, Alison, may I present Paul, who is very much into spanking. Why don't you let him know what days you'll be coming to us and he can plan his next visit accordingly," suggested Hildegarde pleasantly.

"Friday and Saturday nights for sure," mused Brooke, upsetting David. "And probably a weekday afternoon or two as well."

"I'll definitely be in," Paul promised.

"Meanwhile, Cherry is here and I have Hope visiting for the entire night," Hildegarde consoled the spanker before jumping up to answer the door.

"Can we go now?" David demanded, causing a shudder to run through Brooke.

"Are you going to buy me dinner?"

"Dinner? Sure. Of course," he was taken aback by her complete lack of embarrassment at the entire situation and found himself continually readjusting his attitude toward his ex-student.

"And what about my birthday spanking?" she asked as he led her out the door.

"Don't worry about that!" David promised.

Because he hadn't spent any money at the club David took Brooke to an expensive French restaurant, where she was served wine without question. With her tall, elegant carriage, sophisticated dress and high heels, she might have passed for twenty-one.

Brooke was as happy as love, success and promise could make a girl. Her guiltless exuberance was attractive yet frightening to David.

"Tell me about you and that fairy princess at the club," Brooke demanded over dessert.

"If I give you my cake, can I avoid answering that question?" David asked, pushing a chocolate lacquered pyramid across the table to her.

"I want to know about my rival."

"Your what?"

"My competitor."

"Brooke, what's gotten into you?"

"Nothing. I'm just staking my claim."

"That wine must be going to your head," he declared, amazed at her boldness.

"What's the matter, Mr. Lawrence, don't you want Betty and Veronica fighting over you?"

"Certainly not."

"We don't have to fight. We can do a split shift."

"You're talking out of turn, young lady," he growled, both shocked and aroused by her self-confidence.

"Oh, yeah? What are you going to do about it?"

"I think there's only one thing to do– take you home and spank you."

Brooke had not the slightest hesitation about being alone with her ex-teacher, who took her home to a pleasant guesthouse on Amor Drive. In fact, she longed to surrender to him as soon as possible. But as he locked the door, adjusted the lights and gave her a long, cool look, she suddenly remembered the remarks she had made at dinner and wondered if he thought her very rude.

"I suppose I did speak out of turn," she confessed shyly.

"Having second thoughts about coming?"

"Oh, no. Never. You must have figured out how much I care."

"I did nothing of the sort. You think I sit around daydreaming about my students?"

"No, but after the incident last Spring..."

"Oh, that. I see your point. Well, yes, I admit I did think about you quite a bit after that, but only in the context of my job being jeopardized by your infernal snooping and video taping."

"Oh, I see, you're too pure and noble to ever think about a girl student, is that it?"

"No, that is not it, you fresh brat. I never claimed to be either pure or noble. Far from it. I'm just not attracted to teenaged girls. Now, I know that may come as a shock to you, but it happens to be a very good trait in a high school teacher."

"I see. I have to get older before I can become interesting to you."

"I didn't say that. You may be the exception." David smiled. "You certainly don't act like any teenaged girl I've ever met before."

"Thanks!"

David's house was decorated in the pastel-hued, spare, uncomfortable Southwestern style. Thus, Brooke was led into a nook with peach washed walls, which contained a distressed plank table and four sturdy, wooden chairs. One of these was pulled out and David sat. He then pulled her down across his lap.

"Tell me what kind of spanking you've been thinking about," he demanded, smoothing her short, shiny skirt down and running his palm across her slim, upper thighs.

"The silver screen kind."

"You mean, just over your skirt?"

"For starters."

"How many smacks?"

"You're asking me?"

"How hard?"

"You decide."

"I don't want to hurt you."

"You won't."

"Oh? You mean someone has done this before?"

"Willie has spanked me," she admitted.

"Willie!" David didn't have to pretend indignation. "You granted that callous youth the divine privilege of turning you over his knee?" Smack! David's hand came down. Smack! And then once again on the other cheek. "I'm appalled," he added, unleashing a stinging volley of spanks that caused Brooke to yip.

"But, he was my boyfriend," Brooke pointed out. "Ouch! You have a hard hand, Mr. Lawrence," she added, with out rancor. When she reached back to rub he caught it and pinned it to her side before continuing the spanking.

"If you want to work for Hildegarde you're going to have to learn to take much harder spankings than this without making a fuss," he informed her, rapidly warming the back of her skirt with sharp, measured smacks.

"I wasn't complaining," she hastened to explain.

"You'd better not complain, after the anxiety you've put me through!" Now David began to fully express his resentment against Brooke for tracking him down at The Keep seven months before. He pulled up her PVC skirt, carefully tugged down her expensive seamed pantyhose and snapped the black satin g-string she had on underneath. "Lesson #1," he told her, slapping her hard after every remark for emphasis, once on each cheek, "you don't go out to play with a spanking person in pantyhose and a g-string!"

"But this skirt is too short for a garter belt," she confessed after catching her breath, for his hand felt much harder on her bare bottom. Now he yanked her g-string down and spanked her several dozen times more.

"Then the skirt is too short to go out in," he declared. "You want to be mistaken for a hooker?"

"I got this jumper at the hottest shop on Melrose," she protested, wriggling on his lap.

"I say the dress is too short. Are you arguing with me?" he demanded.

"No," she replied.

"And wear regular panties next time," he ordered.

"Is there going to be a next time?"

"I mean next time you go out with a spanking person," he replied coolly.

"Oh."

"That reminds me," he renewed his grip on her waist and brought his hand down hard on her already pinkened, peaches and creamy bottom, "I didn't like that fresh remark you made about staking your claim." Now he spanked her even more emphatically. Brooke took it as long as she could, but finally burst into sobs.

"What are you doing?" he stopped spanking her and took a look at her face. He'd never spanked a girl to tears before and it gave him a terrible thrill.

"I'm not sorry I did that," he told her, lifting her off his lap and helping her to set her clothes to rights. "You had a real one coming for all sorts of reasons."

"I know," she replied, as meekly as it was possible for her to be.

"Naturally, I never meant to make you cry," he added, searching her face for a clue to her real state of mind.

She merely rubbed her bottom and returned his gaze wide-eyed.

"You see how disagreeable I can be when someone irritates me," David tossed off casually as he lit a cigarette.

"I don't blame you," she told him.

"No?"

"Oh, no. You have every right to be annoyed with me. Because I'm such an egotist, I never considered the fact that you might be truly indifferent to me. I apologize."

"Come off it, Brooke, I hate false humility. I've never been indifferent to you for a second and you know it."

"Then how do you feel about me?"

"You scare the hell out of me."

"I'm really harmless," she assured him with a smile.

"Yeah?" he laughed.

"May I have a cigarette?"

"You don't smoke."

"I started."

"You ought to know better," he observed, lighting her a cigarette.

"So, are we going to play again?" she asked shyly.

"I don't know. I want to talk to a lawyer first."

"But I'm eighteen now."

"You're also a recent ex-student of mine, which could damage my reputation, and possibly lead to my dismissal. And what kind of references could I expect if I were fired under those circumstances?"

"I see that I'm getting the brush-off," she commented.

"Honey, it's not like that. But a man in my position has to be more careful than the average player in the scene."

"I see. The man I worshiped has no backbone!" Brooke said angrily.

"You must want another spanking," he replied, unruffled.

"I might as well, since it's the last time I'll be seeing you."

"Look," he told her, taking her by her forearm and pulling her against him, "you'll see me whenever I tell you to come over here. Understand?" Then he kissed her.

The next day was Saturday and as on most recent Saturdays, David's first order of business was calling on Hope at her tiny, fifth floor apartment on Franklin Street, Hollywood, to see if she needed help with any errands. He found her in her favorite position, in front of her mirror, planning her morning outfit. She was in a robe of white merino wool, her small feet thrust into matching slippers with embroidered toes. Next to her was fresh ground coffee. Propped up against the mirror was Elle. Laid out on a nearby chair was a short denim jumper and white tee shirt. It was a warm day for November and Hope planned to do some shopping. She was deciding between well-behaved flats and open toed, sling back, 4" pumps when David entered with his usual offering of rose buds.

"I didn't expect to see you for some time!" Hope cried, jumping up to throw her arms around his neck.

"Why not?" He looked puzzled.

"Well, you did leave with Brooke last night," Hope pouted.

"Well, it was her birthday."

"And I suppose she got her birthday spanking?"

"Yes."

"And what else?"

"A kiss. She's only eighteen, you know."

"Whereas I'm all of twenty-five," Hope said, sitting on his lap and nuzzling his ear. "You need have no reservations with me, my darling."

"Thanks," he tightened his arms around her waist.

"You know, we haven't played since I left The Keep," she reminded him, squirming on his lap in a way that aroused him acutely.

"I know. But I did bring allowance today," he told her.

"That's nice, but not necessary. In fact, I'd almost rather hand you money now and then, you dear, underpaid public servant. "

"That arrangement wouldn't suit me, my little working girl," he told her firmly, divesting himself of his jacket and moving a good armless chair into the center of her studio.

David took Hope over his knee and spanked her as he always did at The Keep. He began over her robe and gave her a good warm up, then pulled it up to discover that she had nothing on underneath.

As usual, her silken skin colored quickly under his hand. And as usual, fifteen minutes into the session, Hope began to reveal her accessibility and excitement. But as usual, when she arched to his hand, he ignored the invitation, refusing to touch her intimately. And with her usual frustration, Hope wondered why.

"David?"

"Yes, dear?" he paused to rub away the sting.

"Don't you like girls?'

"What?"

"Don't you like me?"

"What a question. You're one of my favorite things in life."

"Then why do you always spank me so prudishly?" Hope sprang off his lap. "Are you not into sex?"

David flushed. "Of course I'm into sex. But not with someone I'm paying for a session."

First she gasped with indignation, then hot tears filled her eyes. Drawing herself up to her full five feet and five inches of lithe femininity, Hope deliberately slapped him, albeit very lightly, across the face.

"Is that all you think of me?" she cried.

"I think the world of you, that's why I wouldn't insult you by expecting your favors for a hundred bucks," he replied angrily, for he also had a quick temper and disliked being slapped, even lightly.

"Insult me? Don't you think you insult me every time I invite you to touch me and you ignore me?"

"I was attempting to behave respectfully," David frostily replied.

"It's a safe sex thing, isn't it? You think I'm some sort of high risk slut, don't you?"

"Certainly not. Everyone knows you're a princess."

"They do?" Hope smiled briefly with relief.

"I'm probably a lot more of a slut than you are," David tantalized her. "Anyway, I always use a rubber, so that's not the point."

"Well, what is? You're not in love with Brooke, are you?"

"Of course not. She's even less suitable than you are."

"Don't tell me you only go out with other academics," Hope protested.

"Not exactly."

"You don't think I'm smart enough for you!"

"You're plenty smart, but you're also a B&D call girl. You think I want my girlfriend running out at all hours to do sessions with strange men? Or making fetish videos?"

Hope began to cheer up when she realized he had given this some consideration before deciding to act like an idiot.

"Why not? You often told me at the club that you liked to spank me after two or three other men had warmed me up. Now you're playing the Puritan," she reminded him.

"That's a good point," he granted.

"If you wanted to keep things impersonal between us, you shouldn't have begun coming to see me like this. Why, the way you're always offering to perform chores and do favors for me, is it any wonder I got the wrong idea about your intentions?" she demanded haughtily, shrewdly targeting the one area in which he was genuinely culpable.

"Look, isn't there some way we could still be friends and play without getting involved? I mean, I thought that was the beauty of doing sessions," he protested weakly.

"Oh, you make me sick. Get out. And don't come back!" she ordered, throwing the allowance at him. "You stupid, conventional, hung-up, impotent, high school teacher!"

David stared at her for a moment, more impressed by her ability to tell him off so succinctly than hurt by her accusations.

"All right," he snapped at length. "You asked for it and now you're going to get it. Get over here." He took her in his arms and kissed her on the mouth for the first time.

She went limp, then clung to him, astonished at the depth of his kiss.

Then David pulled her robe off and looked at her completely nude body for the first time. "Slap my face, will you?" He gave her a shake, wound his hand in her hair and kissed her again. Then, because she weighed nearly nothing, he picked her up and carried her to the day bed.

"Face down," he told her, taking off his belt. "You're getting six of the best for that smack in the face."

"You deserved it," she replied defiantly.

"I said face down."

Hope obeyed with a pout. The belt came down hard and fast across her bare bottom six times. She hardly had a chance to gasp between each whack. Number three brought tears to her eyes and by six she was sobbing. When he was finished he threw his belt aside and pulled her around to face him.

"I've got a better way to punish you for that crack about impotence," he told her coolly, but wiped her face dry with his handkerchief. Then he took her over to a green leather spanking horse, which was the only piece of play furniture in the tiny flat, and bent her over one end.

She turned to him and asked, "Are you telling me you have a rubber in your pocket this instant?"

"Worried?" he asked insolently, pushing her head back down. "Just behave yourself like the submissive you're supposed to be."

Hope gave a nearly inaudible groan of surrender at the new tone in his voice. She turned to see a zipper come down, a large cock emerge and a rubber come out. Once the truncheon was properly sheathed, he let it rest between her cheeks and reached around to capture and lightly squeeze her breast. She ground back against him with her bottom and arched her sex up.

"Since you're so impatient..." he spread her and nudged into her lightly, but she was extremely small and he pulled away. "You're not nearly wet enough," he told her, spanking her bottom and fingering her pussy until she was. He had never touched her like this before and she could only whimper and pant her encouragement. "How aggressive you were today," he scolded. "My little Princess demanding sex!" He slapped her inner thighs until she squirmed. "Is that the way a perfect submissive is supposed to behave?"

"I suppose not," she conceded. Her soft response was rewarded by five or six light, sharp smacks on her parted sex. She arched up a little more to show him how agreeable this felt. He went around to one side of her, tucked one arm under her waist, lifted her off the horse an inch or two and spanked her damp pubic mound and labia even more firmly.

"You couldn't wait for our romance to take its course and for me to approach you in the proper way at the proper time, could you?"

"I'm sorry," she murmured as he let her back down and went around behind her again.

"Did it ever occur to you that you may have opened Pandora's Box?" he suggested, penetrating her slowly, with his hands fastened to her waist.

"What do you mean?" she gasped as he thoroughly filled her.

"Now that I've had you like this, do you think I'm going to be satisfied just to spank you and lace your corsets?"

"I hope not, my darling," she breathed.

"Got any lube?"

"What for?" she turned her head.

"What do you think?"

"Isn't this a little sudden?" she squeaked, barely able to accommodate him in the proper place.

"Not to me; I've been daydreaming about sodomizing you for six months," he confessed, spreading and examining her bottom.

"Can't I have six months to dream about it too?"

"You can have six minutes," he told her, withdrawing to abandon her and search for the lube. "And don't move, unless you want the strap again," he warned her.

Upon his return he found her pacing and nervously smoking one of his cigarettes. He relieved her of it with a smile. "Worried?" Now he bent her back over the horse and went to work with the lube, fingering her deeply in both places until she sighed and ground against the leather. Then he only fingered her bottom and slapped it in the middle of it. "Your six minutes are up, bad girl." When Hope only whimpered in reply he spread her and took her, like an expert in the tricky art of sodomy, giving them both an orgasm in a matter of a few short minutes.

"You brute," she whimpered, for form's sake. "No one's ever done that to me before."

"Really?"

As she turned to see him smile there came a knock on the door.

"You expecting some one?" he unceremoniously extracted his still throbbing cock from her tighter than ever sheath and disappeared into the bathroom to dispose of the evidence and put himself back together.

"Only Brooke," Hope replied, pulling her robe back on and answering the door without concern.

"Brooke! What are you doing here?" David demanded as Hope let her in.

"We're going shopping on Melrose. Didn't I tell you?" Hope linked arms with the willowy brunette, who smiled down at her and then across at David.

"So you're going through with this, are you?" David frowned at his ex-student.

"Through with what?" Brooke replied.

"The Betty and Veronica thing."

"Nonsense, Mr. Lawrence, we've simply realized how much we have in common," Brooke explained.

"And think of the impact we'll make as a tag team," Hope suggested blithely, squeezing Brooke's long waist. David did and it made him shudder.

"I'll just jump into these," Hope reported, taking her pre-selected outfit into the bathroom to dress.

Alone with David, Brooke wasn't quite so cocky and indeed avoided his gaze.

"I still say you're too young for any of this," he grouched.

"And I still say I'm into B&D and always have been."

"Well, if something awful happens, don't say I didn't warn you."

"Something awful could have happened to you when I discovered your secret life. But it didn't."

"Your point being?"

"My point being, preach what you practice, Mr. Lawrence."

"Don't be smart," he snapped and Brooke had the grace to blush. Still annoyed at the interruption of his first sexual tryst with Hope, he frowned at Hildegarde's newest protégée. Then he put his jacket on and crammed his grey fedora down on his head. "I'll be going now," he announced as Hope emerged fully dressed.

"You don't want to take us to brunch?" Hope asked, astonished at his eagerness to deprive himself of their company.

"No, I do not want to take you to brunch," he returned, with an edge to his voice that made the girls stare at each other. "Good-bye!" was his final word to them before clattering down the five flights of stairs.

"What did we do?" Hope wondered.

"Maybe it's a sensory overload thing," Brooke speculated as they leaned over the railing to follow the descending felt hat.

"You're probably right," Hope agreed, "in the past twenty-four hours he's spanked you for the first time, had me for the first time and now he's just found out we're determined to be friends. No wonder he's confused."

"He seemed more hostile than confused," Brooke observed.

"Well, that's to his credit. Could you respect a man who wasn't slightly unnerved by a situation like this?"

"Still, he might at least have offered us a ride to Melrose."

"Never mind, he brought me plenty of allowance. We can take cabs, have lunch and even buy stockings."

"And let's not forget a present for Mr. Lawrence," Brooke suggested, training her video lens on Hope's radiance for the first time.

"Mr. Lawrence doesn't accept presents from ladies," Hope declared, establishing an immediate relationship with Brooke's camera.

"Nor apparently does he take them to brunch."

"It's better this way," said Hope, "we can talk about him all afternoon." They ran downstairs and followed David out into the brilliant sunlight.

Chapter Three

Life With Hope

In the midst of a February snowstorm, David and Hope Spencer Lawrence, lodged in an old sedan, drove down the cobble stoned streets of Random Point for the first time. David steered with one hand and kept his other arm around Hope, who snuggled against him.

He was an English teacher, late of Hollywood High, 37 and well favored, with a sparkle in his eyes that girls loved. His dazzling bride, twelve years his junior, had been until the previous week, L.A.'s most popular working submissive. He'd met her as a client, patronized her for months and finally fell in love.

The marriage had been David's brainstorm, after the offer of an instructor's position at an eastern prep school arrived. It was too fine an opportunity to refuse, but the prospect of abandoning Hope was not a happy one. The best solution seemed to be to bring her along as his wife.

"How are you at budgeting?" David asked, for their new life together would be nothing like the old.

"Oh David, you're so funny. You know I'm always broke."

"Then you might want to think about getting a little job," he suggested, noticing a help wanted sign in the window of an elegant lingerie shop.

"Darling, I fully intended to, but that vacancy looks more interesting," said Hope peering at the intriguing frontage of Marguerite Alexander's bookshop, whose window also bore a help wanted sign, along with a small blue neon invitation to cappuccino and tea cakes.

"A bookstore? What about references?"

"Oh, I'm sure I won't need them."

"Why do you think that?"

"I never have."

"Are you saying you'll be hired on looks alone?" he bristled.

"Why bother raising an eyebrow? I didn't make up the rules of life," she blithely replied.

"You'd better start soft peddling those West Coast conceits from now on," he warned, "we're in New England now and they don't tolerate goddesses here."

"I figured as much when I noticed the pillory in the town square," she casually brushed off the scolding.

They parked and hurried into the Victorian triple-decker that housed the bookshop. A wood burning fireplace warmed the coffee bar to which the tweed coated beauty migrated. While David was freshening up, Hope ordered lattes and watched them being prepared by a striking young man, roughly thirty years of age, to whom she felt an immediate attraction. When she handed him the money he smiled back at her, admiring her two feet of natural corn silk hair.

"I love your shop," Hope murmured.

"Thank you." She also loved his jet-black hair and pure white skin.

"My husband and I are new here in town."

"Oh, really?" His mellifluous voice gave her pleasure.

"He's going to be teaching at Braemar."

"That's fine! Are you a teacher too?"

Hope chortled. "No, in fact I was just going to ask you whether I might apply for the clerk job you have advertised."

"You want to work here?" the young man seemed amazed.

"I love bookstores and I've always longed to be a librarian. It's been my fantasy since childhood," she confided.

"Really!" Sloan remarked in disbelief.

"I only need a pocket money job."

"That's an accurate description of the salary," he reported.

"May I fill out an application?"

"You really want to work here?"

"I have the cutest cherry apron I could wear while preparing cappuccinos," she disclosed with excitement. "Oh, and all sorts of skirts and cardigans for rainy days."

"When can you start?"

Hope rejoined David and set the coffees down, announcing, "I got the job."

David's disbelief was short-lived as he scrutinized the savvy young man behind the counter.

"That's my new boss, Sloan Taylor. Isn't he nice?"

Hearing his name mentioned, Sloan came over to shake David's hand and introduce himself. He gave them helpful information on finding the inn where they were to stay that night and the rental agent who would lead them to the house on Pigeon Cove the following day.

When they emerged from the shop the wind had ceased to whine but snow continued to fall. David waited until they got into the car to demand, "Hope, did you flirt with Mr. Taylor?"

"No!" she protested, a thrill.

"Then how did you get the job so fast?"

"When I said I was the new school teacher's wife he knew I would be perfect for the bookstore."

"That almost makes sense," David mused.

"Besides, anyone could tell that I'd be good for business."

David shook his head disapprovingly.

"You're really awfully conceited."

She blushed but ignored the censure. Instead she began to mentally unpack and search for the perfect outfit to wear for her first day at work.

As they stepped up to the registration desk at the Bone and Feather Inn a few minutes later Hope cried, "Oh, David, ask for the honeymoon suite!"

The suite was in the attic, up many flights of narrow stairs. The rewards were a hearth and an antique oak bed.

"Where did you get this?" David asked, pouring them each a shot of brandy from the complimentary bottle on the sideboard and eyeing the cover of the New Rod magazine that Hope had tossed on the bed.

"That was on a rack at the book shop. And you'll notice it gets published right here in Random Point!" She lit his cigarette then curled up in the window seat with her snifter.

"I can't wait to visit the publisher."

"Visit him why?"

"Well, I am in the Scene, after all. I should think he'd want to meet me. Maybe he'll give me modeling work."

David flipped through the spanking magazine lingeringly. Finally he said, "B&D modeling is not an appropriate vocation for a prep school teacher's wife."

"Oh, come on, David. It's the millennium. Nobody cares."

"I care!" he corrected her emphatically. Hope felt her face become warm. The next moment tears filled her eyes. She slipped into the bathroom before he could notice.

While the antique copper tub filled with hot water she suppressed several heartfelt sobs at the injustice of it all. He'd found her through the Scene, the Scene had infused romance into his life and now he wanted to coldly extract her from it! Of course she understood it wasn't jealousy, but fear for his reputation. As he'd pointed out, they weren't in Hollywood anymore. Still it hurt that he could snap at her like that. Even though she felt excited by it too.

Sinking down into the bath, Hope mutinously fantasized about her delicious new boss Sloan Taylor turning her over his knee, spanking her soundly, then bending her over a reading table and taking her completely from behind. She'd noticed David notice just how good-looking Sloan was. His pretty boy hackles had risen. He was used to being the only handsome man in her life. How thrilling would be the coming of Spring.

The next morning David got the keys to Cobweb Cottage from the agent while Hope took her first walk around Random Point. The snowstorm had blown out and it was overcast and very cold.

Her first stop was Hugo Sands' Antiques. The shop was empty, its proprietor sequestered in his office when the doorbell tinkled. He emerged in a moment, a sophisticated male of forty-eight. Hope smiled and he smiled back.

"Good day," he said.

"Mr. Hugo Sands?"

"Yes."

"I'm Hope Lawrence. I'm going to be working for Mr. Taylor across the street."

"How nice!" Hugo did not exaggerate his pleasure, for she was divinely fair.

"But the reason I came over is that I just saw your magazine for the first time and I wanted to tell you how much I love it," she declared with complete candor and a total lack of embarrassment.

"Is this true?" Hugo asked in great surprise, more charmed by his angelic visitor every moment.

"Oh, of course. I'm a player myself," she proudly declared.

"My dear Miss Lawrence, you're bowling me over."

"It's been Mrs. Lawrence for the past three days. I wish I could pose for you, but my husband doesn't think that would be appropriate, considering his new teaching appointment at Braemar," she revealed regretfully.

"One can see his point."

"I can't tell you how happy I am to discover Random Point is a Scene town."

"Is your husband a player as well?"

"Absolutely," she beamed. "In fact he found me at The Keep in Hollywood."

"I've heard of that club. So, you were working there?"

"Sure."

"Dom or sub?"

"Sub."

"Bondage or spanking?"

"Why, both!"

"I'll have to give a party to welcome you two," said Hugo.

"You will? How nice you are!"

Hope spent some time being shown around the shop by Hugo. Then she lingered in the back with her host becoming lusciously stoned on eye watering weed. Trundling back to the inn she was stunned to note that ninety minutes had passed since her sally out into the village streets and that David was drinking Irish coffee in the pub with as cross an expression as she had ever seen on his patrician face.

"Where the hell have you been?" he demanded. "I've been waiting for hours!" He marched out to the car and she followed meekly, explaining that she had been touring the village.

"Is that all?" He slammed both their doors getting in. "Are you sure you didn't get side tracked by someone or thing?"

"Yes, dear."

"Just wait till I get you alone in that isolated cottage!" he promised terribly, throwing the car into gear and pulling away from the inn.

"Why?" she asked with wide eyes.

"Why do you think? Because I'm going to spank the living daylights out of you!"

"David, no!" she protested, her wide, red mouth forming a ravishing pout. "That's not your way."

"It is from now on."

"But, that's just for playing, isn't it?"

"Who says?"

In a moment they were out on the coast road driving towards their new home a few miles away.

"I'm not getting out of the car unless you promise to be sweet," she declared over folded arms as he came to a halt in front of the rustic cottage.

"Oh yes you are," he told her firmly, opening her door and pulling her out. For a moment they both stared at the churning, slate blue waters of the cove, then up at the white sky, filled with dipping, cawing gulls.

"Gosh, darling, are we really getting all this for a twelve hundred a month?" she cried in disbelief, ignoring the biting cold.

"The realtor said it was small," David explained, also mesmerized. Then he purposefully led her inside. She broke away from him to examine their new surroundings. There was a kitchen with a cellar and pantry, a bedroom that connected to an attic and a small sitting room with a hearth. She bounced on the four-poster, tried the rocking chair, admired herself in the cheval glass and approved of the storage space. The agent had turned on the heat and arranged for the basic utilities.

"It's so cute," Hope breathed.

"So are you, but that won't save you this time," he grabbed her velvet earlobe and pulled her over to the first proper chair he saw, sat down and turned her over his knee. Pulling off her woolen reefer coat and tossing it aside, he wrapped one hand around her waist and brought the other one down on her bottom. Her snug beige leggings offered some protection from his fast descending palm, but each resounding smack was firmly felt and made her squirm.

Hope tried to struggle free; perversely offended by the way she had been summarily seized. "This is outrageous!" she cried. "Just because I got caught up inspecting my new environment! Ouch!"

"I don't like being kept waiting." Smack! Smack! Smack!

"I can't believe you're really spanking me!" she whimpered. "It's just too retrograde!"

"Get used to it, or wise up," told her, finishing with a dozen of the best and pushing her off his lap. Hope rubbed her punished bottom through her leggings, feeling how nicely they kept in the heat. "Why darling, you're blushing," he accused her, now pulling her down on his lap the right way around and burying his face in her perfumed hair. She allowed him to enfold her in his arms but sat perfectly still, her own arms folded in apparent pique. But her resolve was not proof against his lips upon her throat and she soon began to wriggle.

"I never dreamed that I had entered into a lifestyle relationship," she intoned disapprovingly.

"It wouldn't have to be if you could learn to behave," he advised her, lighting a cigarette and taking a turn around the rooms. A knock came at the door and Hope rushed to answer it.

An extremely attractive brunette, around Hope's age, in a navy toggle coat and Basque beret, stood on the threshold of the cottage bearing groceries.

"Hi! I'm Laura Random. Hugo said that you were moving in today and suggested I deliver some provisions. There's supposed to be a tremendous snowstorm later and you may not want to go out."

"Hugo?" David looked at Hope questioningly.

"Hugo Sands, the publisher," she whispered, "of the cute magazine. Remember we read it together last night?"

"When did you meet him?"

"Earlier today."

"You didn't mention that," David snapped before pleasantly conducting introductions and thanking their new neighbor for her kindness.

"My best friend used to live here," said Laura, putting away the milk, butter, eggs, coffee, tea, sugar, bread and jam that she had brought. "You can hear the surf pounding all night."

"Glorious," Hope murmured.

"I hear you're newlyweds."

"Yes!" Hope was thrilled to assent.

"It's splendid to have a new Scene couple in town!" Laura declared.

David looked at his wife reproachfully.

"David, Hugo and Laura are utterly cool," Hope explained hastily. "After all, they publish that delightful magazine. If I couldn't tell them, who could I tell?"

"You weren't supposed to tell anyone," David growled.

Laura stared at him wide-eyed as Hope felt her face grow warm. David lit a cigarette as the girls exchanged a glance. To change the subject Hope asked Laura whether she had ever seen a pair of 8" fetish pumps. The girls went out to the car to look for the suitcase that contained Hope's shoes.

"Why is David upset?" Laura asked as they lugged the heavy suitcase back between them.

"He thinks his new position at Braemar will require a lower profile then when he only taught at Hollywood High."

"Were you not supposed to tell us that you worked at The Keep?"

"I guess not." Hope looked momentarily guilty, but quickly shook off the unaccustomed sensation.

"Don't forget to call me if you need a ride anywhere while David is away," Laura insisted as she departed a few minutes later.

"I'm so close to the village, I'll just hitch one if I need it," Hope declared.

"You'll do no such thing!" David cried, horror-struck.

"Please call me instead," Laura said. "I live just a mile down the road. Good-bye Mr. Lawrence. It was very nice meeting you."

"Thanks for coming by," he shook her pretty hand.

"Thank you for bringing me a new girlfriend," said Laura, exiting. "We'll have a party soon."

"Party?" David questioned Hope when Laura left.

"They apparently feel that us moving into town is sufficient reason to throw a party."

"They?"

"The Random Point Scene people."

"Hope?"

"Yes, dear?"

"You kept me waiting for one and one half hours at the Bone and Feather Inn, in order to enjoy a protracted tête-à-tête with a decadent dominant male."

Hope refused to meet his eyes.

"You lied to me, concealed facts, and for all I know, played with Mr. Sands this fine day!"

"Of course I did nothing of the sort!" Hope cried, deeply affronted, in spite of having amiably accepted a stingy birching from Hugo Sands in his office.

"And how dare you even talk about hitching a ride? My blood runs cold at the thought. Believe me, young lady, if I ever do catch you hitching, I'll give you the worst licking of your life!" David threatened.

"Then I won't let you catch me," she retorted, sauntering into the bedroom with the 8" pumps still in her hands.

"Oh, are you gonna get it," David promised, mostly under his breath, while following her in and commenting aloud, "I don't believe I've ever seen you in those shoes before. Why don't you put them on for me, darling?'

"I'd be thrilled to!" she cried, always eager to model anything, no less such extraordinary examples of high fetish couture.

"But not with the leggings," he urged her, lighting the antique cast iron stove. Flushed with excitement, Hope tore off her sweater, leggings and sox and hunted for a garter belt and stockings while he looked for his hairbrush. Her fifties-style panties and bra displayed a classic form that was enhanced by her waist length hair.

"Won't you help me?" she asked, sitting on the bed and extending her slim, pretty feet. David sat beside her and carefully fastened eight tiny buckles across the instep of each of the fantastically high-heeled shoes, then helped her to her feet. Hope tottered gracefully across the room on the 8" heels while David watched amazed.

"Sit here," he told her, lifting her to sit on a high stool by the stove. "Give me your wrists," he said, pulling a handkerchief out of his jacket pocket and taking her by the hands.

"Why?" she laughed uncertainly, consciously tensing her wrists while he bound them together rudimentarily in front of her. "Now lean forward," he ordered, "and brace yourself against the seat with your hands."

"Why?"

"Because it will cause your bottom to protrude ever so nicely."

"But, haven't I been spanked enough?"

"Don't make me laugh, dear."

"Not the hair brush!" she cried when she saw him pick it up.

"You'd better sit still, honey," he recommended, "that stool is a bit rickety and between the 8" heels and your wrists being bound, I wouldn't count on your usual balance."

"You diabolical brute! You only put me in these shoes so that I wouldn't be able to escape!"

"You're smart!"

"David, please, you're scaring me."

"Oh, I'm sorry," he protested insincerely, slipping one arm around her waist to hold her in place while he used the back of the brush to smack her jutting cheeks.

"Ouch! That really hurts!" she cried, wriggling on the stool. After administering one dozen firm swats he tossed the brush aside and pulled her panties down to where her bottom met the seat of the stool. Her fair skin was pink where he'd spanked her. She tried for a glimpse but he turned her head front wards. Then he picked the stool up with Hope still perched upon it and set it down in the corner, with Hope's back toward the room. She turned to pout at him as he lit a cigarette.

"Turn around," he ordered.

"I won't sit in the corner!" she protested.

"You really have no choice," he pointed out the folly of attempting to jump down off the stool in the 8" heels with her wrists still bound.

"Isn't this a bit of a busman's holiday?"

"I wish, but realistically teachers haven't sent kids to the corner since shortly before I was born."

"How long do I have to stay here?"

"I haven't decided yet, but if I hear one more complaint I'll put you in a much worse position."

Hope bit her lip, intrigued. Then she began to wriggle her panties back up.

"What do you think you're doing?'

"Restoring my modesty."

"Nothing doing," he insisted, striding across the room to lift her from the stool, then turn and bend her over it, so that the seat supported her tummy while she gripped and stepped upon its rungs for additional support. Now her head was down and her buttocks uppermost, with her panties still down.

"Hope's Honeymoon Spanking, Scene Two," he commented, paddling her upturned cheeks.

"Ow! This isn't fair. I like to be comfortable for my spankings," she cried. "And not unduly embarrassed."

"Tsk. That's too bad," he commiserated, deliberately probing her vagina with deft fingers. "But that's the price you pay for being so bad."

Now he held her down against the stool and administered dozens of hard smacks.

When he paused to survey the pinkness and light a cigarette Hope raised her head. "Wouldn't you like some fresh ground coffee to go with that? And even scrambled eggs and toast?"

"I did say you were smart," he commented, lifting her off the stool and carrying her into the kitchen before setting her down on the stilt like shoes. "Do you think you could manage like this?"

"Oh, you mean I'm not to change my shoes?" She pulled her panties up with difficulty.

He untied her wrists. "No."

"Very well, but you'll have to stay close by me," she stipulated, tottering to the counter where Laura had deposited the provisions. "And I must have my cherry apron as well."

David got her dark red cotton apron, slipped it over her head and tied it around her waist. Watching her teeter and sway around the kitchen was amusing enough to make up for the time he'd been kept waiting earlier in the day.

"A man could forgive much in a wife capable of scrambling eggs this perfectly," he complimented her some twenty minutes later as she leaned across him to fill his coffee cup, presenting her pantied bottom peeking out between the two apron halves in back. He patted her and straightened her stocking seams.

"A man will have much to forgive," she predicted, wedging herself into the window seat to unbuckle her shoes. "Luckily I know several dozen recipes."

David lectured Hope as they drove to the faculty tea on Saturday afternoon.

"Don't talk about B&D at all, but especially don't tell anyone that you were a pro."

"Okay, darling."

"Say you used to do public relations for the Hollywood Chamber of Commerce. It's plausible and not entirely untrue," he recommended, pulling into the long wooded drive that lead to Braemar.

"Aces," she agreed, checking her hair in a mirror. She'd tied it back with a velvet ribbon for a demurely romantic effect. Her skirt, blouse and cardigan were exact replicas of those worn by Hope Lange in the 1959 career girl film The Best of Everything. Details mattered as she planned to make a great impression on everyone she met.

"And don't talk about sex. You have a propensity for discussing sex in public that I'm going to have to break you of."

"I'll pretend that sex doesn't exist," Hope vowed, marveling at the beauty of the campus blanketed with snow. The overcast sky and moist air promised more precipitation shortly, which thrilled the erstwhile sun babe.

"And don't talk about clothes. Or Hollywood celebrities."

"Not even ones that have been dead a minimum of 30 years?"

"I suppose that classic cinema would constitute an acceptable topic of conversation," he conceded.

"That's a relief, because we were beginning to run out of things I could talk about," Hope remarked good-naturedly.

"Let's see, have I forgotten anything? Oh yes, don't flirt with the men. Faculty spouses don't do that. For that matter, don't flirt with the women either."

"What if there's an obvious lesbian who likes me?"

"If she makes the first overture, okay."

"Right."

"I guess that's about it. Think you can do it?'

"Piece of cake."

The main parlor was gilded in ornate mid-Victorian style, with handsome portraits and a marble hearth. Hope watched fresh snow fall on the woods through the tall, velvet-curtained windows while relishing her tea and watercress sandwiches.

To make the situation even more piquant, she recognized Anthony Newton, the composer, at the piano. Hope learned he was a trustee of the school and a local resident! They had already exchanged glances and Hope had smiled. How could she help it when she knew every one of his musical scores by heart? But David had warned her not even to mention a celebrity, no less fawn on one, so she remained in her portion of the room and hoped he would eventually drift her way.

Musing on the charms of the millionaire maestro, Hope was caught unawares when a slim, clean scrubbed, awkwardly dressed thirty-something teacher or teacher's spouse approached her and demanded she sign a petition. Hope smiled and took the proffered clipboard, but paled with horror as she read the petition's intent.

"But I work at Marguerite Alexander's bookshop," Hope protested, handing the clipboard back to the women, whose name badge identified her as Catherine Thaxter-Peake.

"So? Are you telling me you actually approve of the violent, degrading, sadomasochistic literature for sale in its so-called erotic gallery?" returned Catherine.

Hope's heart began to pound as she frantically tried to frame some sort of response of which David would approve.

"But aren't you forgetting freedom of the press?" she shakily replied.

"You mean freedom of the righteously patriarchal American male to exploit, debase and brutalize women! But I wouldn't expect anyone who looked like you to know anything about women's rights," declared Catherine. Now the color flooded Hope's exquisite face in such a way that brought Anthony Newton from the piano to the periphery of the circle. He caught Hope's eye and smiled. Gratified, Hope confronted her attacker.

"I know that women have the right to express their own sexuality," she declared, "and certainly more than half the authors in our gallery are female."

"They're sick, deluded. It's disgusting. It should be banned!" the woman cried, becoming severely agitated by Hope's stubborn refusal to agree. Redness instantly rimmed Catherine Thaxter-Peake's eyes as they clouded with tears of frustration. Hysteria raised her pitch as she continued to renounce the huge collection of dominant/submissive erotica that contributed to the unique character of Marguerite Alexander's bookshop. Hope felt choked by disappointment at Catherine's refusal to acknowledge the validity of sexuality opposite to her own. She guessed that Catherine Thaxter-Peake had been the victim of some unspeakable childhood abuse and felt as if she herself were being asked to share in the guilt, just because she enjoyed being disciplined by refined gentlemen. Then she realized that she was staring into the eyes of a fanatic.

"I recommend you read Camille Paglia," Hope interjected, which caused Catherine Thaxter-Peake to nearly weep with rage.

Seeing that Hope had exhausted her supply of tortured diplomacy Anthony Newton entered the scene.

"May I?" he asked, taking the clipboard out of the woman's hands and quickly looking over the petition.

"Hmmm," he said, nodding with concern as he read on.

"Yes, we need the endorsement of respected members of the artistic community!" cried Catherine, a thrill.

"And I know so many people who would be interested in this too," he stated helpfully. "You should let me take this little task off your hands, Ms. Thaxter-Peake," he offered. "I'm sure you have many other campaigns to keep track of."

"You'd do that?" Catherine was agog.

"Happy to," he blithely agreed, cuddling the petition to his Donegal tweed suit jacket affectionately.

"I must find my husband and tell him. He thought that no one would care. Thank you!" cried Catherine, exiting the room in high spirits.

"Who's her husband?" Hope wondered.

"The P.E. instructor," Anthony reported. Hope's pulse began to return to normal and the tension left her shoulders.

"Thank you for making her go away," Hope murmured, watching with fascination as he tore off the first page of the petition, which bore five or six signatures, crumpled it up and tossed it into the fire.

"Did she upset you?" he asked with concern.

"Look," said Hope, extending her pretty hand to demonstrate how it continued to tremble.

"You handled the situation admirably."

"You're very gallant, Mr. Newton. And I was already your biggest fan."

"I'm a great fan of yours as well."

"Of mine?" Hope queried, puzzled, while suddenly noticing David staring at her from across the room.

"I own four of your videos."

"You own?" Hope reeled.

"So when Hugo Sands told me that an incredibly beautiful creature named Hope Spencer Lawrence had moved to Random Point as the wife of a Braemar instructor, I had to run right over and see if the cameras had done you justice."

"You came over to meet me?" Hope beamed, almost ready to faint from joy at the unexpected recognition and admiration from the Broadway luminary. "But does this mean that you're in the Scene?" she breathed softly.

"Silly. Why else would I own four of your videos?"

"Gosh, Random Point must be some sort of magnet for Scene people. First I meet Hugo Sands and his girlfriend Laura, now you."

"That's just the tip of the iceberg."

"I'm thrilled."

"Hugo said you used to do sessions. Is that still true?"

"Why?"

"I'd love to engage you sometime."

"That sounds heavenly," she cried in spite of her husband's steely gaze that reached across the room. Hope had no idea of whether or not David could hear their conversation and at that moment didn't much care. The important thing was that for the first time in her entire B&D career, which had officially ended with her marriage the week before, she was being courted by a V.I.P.! For a moment she simply bowed her head and basked in the glory of it, thanking the Goddess for all her present blessings.

The next thing she knew, David was beside her telling her that it was time to go. She was led out of the main hall in a pleasurable trance and hardly felt being thrown into the car.

"That Anthony Newton is so nice," she breathed at last before they were half way home.

"You're lucky it's snowing. Otherwise I'd go looking in the woods for a switch."

"To use on me?"

"Damn it, Hope, I specifically asked you not to discuss anything radical and what do I just hear but you arguing with some flaming feminazi about the First Amendment."

"David, you don't understand. She wanted me to sign a hateful petition that directly affected the stock in our store. And when I tactfully protested she began to positively rave. That's when Mr. Newton stepped in. He saw how distressed I was. But believe me darling, I never breathed a word about being in the Scene. Mr. Newton just happened to recognize me from some videos he owns."

David threw her a look. "What's this you're saying now?"

"I know. It's quite amazing. Every other person in Random Point seems to be a player."

"I feel as though I must be dreaming," he admitted. "I had no idea this thing was so widespread."

"It's a small Scene world."

"It didn't seem that way until I met you."

"Yes. I am the key. You should value me, worship me!" She jumped up and down on the seat. David almost smiled. "Instead all you can do is scold me!"

"That's not all I can do."

"I changed your life!"

"I changed yours too."

"That's true." Hope subsided and stared out the window as they drove the coast road to their cottage. "If it weren't for you I'd still be trudging up five flights on Franklin Street, Hollywood and posing for low budget photo shoots in Van Nuys. You and you alone transported me here."

"Now you're talking."

They parked and went inside their cottage. David lit a fire in the parlor hearth while Hope sat opposite on a little padded bench. Then David sat down beside her and took her hand. "Dearest, I thought I asked you not to flirt this afternoon."

"I didn't flirt."

David pulled Hope across his lap. "No?" he patted the seat of her grey tweed straight skirt. "What about Anthony Newton?"

Hope did not reply at once. Then she sighed, "He's dreamy." Frowning, David shrugged off his jacket and rolled up his sleeves. "I'm afraid I might be getting a crush on him," Hope added, in spite of the grip David took on her waist. In reply to this remark he spanked her soundly.

Hope thought, "Mmmm," as she loved being spanked on her skirt. Then just when the heat became a tangible entity, he raised her skirt. Her panties, garter belt and hose were of a silken perfection that matched the flesh they adorned and David felt momentarily humbled by the sudden beauty he beheld. However, he quickly recovered.

"How dare you get a crush on another man when we've been married less than a week?" Now he brought his hand down on her panties hard.

"I'm sure I could get over it if I was permitted to do just one session with him," she suggested hopefully.

"Session?" He paused in spanking her. "You actually had the nerve to talk sessions at the tea today?"

"Mr. Newton brought it up."

David spanked her hard, plainly demonstrating his annoyance. At length he pulled her panties down and off. Her alabaster skin was stained dark pink.

"I am very angry with you, Hope!" he thrilled her by snapping. "You've been a very bad girl, doing everything I told you not to do!" Now he made her feel his indignation with each measured swat.

"Ow! I'm sorry, darling," Hope half-sobbed, honored by his endearing display of jealousy. "But can't you understand?"

"Understand what? That my wife is an attention-addicted little flirt who can't stay faithful to her husband for a week?"

The smacks came steadily for several minutes, hurting more and more.

"But our marriage was so sudden," she protested, "I need time to adjust to the change."

"Don't try to con me. You know you're guilty."

Hope began to feel severely punished and started to cry. David stopped in mid smack and turned her around on his lap. She hid her face against his chest and sobbed, clinging to him.

"Feel better?" he asked presently, still holding her.

"Do you?"

"I always feel better after I've spanked you."

"I'm so glad!" she ground against the ramrod in his trousers. "But do you love me? Really love me?"

"What do you think?" he squeezed her bare bottom under her skirt as she bounced on his lap.

"Can't you say it more romantically than that?" she pouted.

"I suppose that I love you enough to let you do a session now and then," he unexpectedly conceded.

"Darling! That's handsome of you. And if you really want to turn me on, you'll take my money away from me when I get home and beat me soundly for not bringing you more."

"Will that make Baby happy?"

"Yes!"

"I should teach you a lesson and really do it."

"I would orgasm," she vowed. "I love it when you're mean to me."

"I'm never mean to you, you brat," he bristled, tapping her cheek.

"No, of course not, but you do criticize from morning till night, don't you, darling?"

"If I correct you it's for your own good. I'm sure you don't want to sound like an ignorant girl all your life."

"No, Sir," she pressed her head against his chest for comfort.

"Never mind," he soothed her, "in spite of everything, you're very sweet."

Hope loved her new job, but her take-home pay of $296 was spent within an hour of receiving it, on gourmet groceries, small presents for David and a new corset from the exquisite lingerie shop. All the cash that she had brought from California was now gone and she was reluctant to go to her husband for allowance for fear that he would have none to give her until his own payday, several weeks hence. "I can't humiliate him like that," she told herself, "and I won't live on macaroni and cheese! I'd better arrange for that session with Mr. Newton right away!"

Obtaining Anthony's e-mail address from Hugo Sands, Hope began to exchange flirtatious messages with the composer. This went on for a couple of days, during which Anthony induced Hope to discuss her fantasies in detail. Finally he warned her to prepare herself for the session of her life.

Intrigued, Hope begged for particulars, but Anthony only promised that she would enjoy the ordeal in store and be amply recompensed for her time.

The next day Sloan Taylor asked if she might be available on the following Sunday to help him assemble and deliver a consignment of books to the Cliff House, for Mr. Newton's perusal. The queerness of this request made her heart flutter. For why would she be necessary to deliver a box of books?

She could barely sleep for excitement that night, wondering how musical geniuses punished girls. Also, why involve Sloan in the visit, if not to make her most decadent confessed desire come true? Hope couldn't think about it without blushing. A whipping from two men at once. She recalled how interested Anthony had seemed when she'd described this fantasy. Was it possible that Sloan was a good enough friend in the Scene to be included in the session of Hope's life? Reviewing all possible outfits for the following day finally put her to sleep.

As soon as she got to the shop the next afternoon, in a smart little pleated skirt suit and high-heeled oxfords, she began to grill her circumspect boss on what she might expect. But Sloan ignored her questions, packing up the books.

When they arrived at the Cliff House, a petite blonde who might have been Hope's sister opened the door to them. They stared at each other for a moment before recognition dawned. Then Hope cried, "Susan Ross! The only girl who ever made my money go down at The Keep. Even if it was only for three days." They girls embraced.

"I always hoped to meet you again," Susan told her, "in a less competitive environment." The girls linked arms and Susan led them upstairs to the third floor studio. As they walked in Anthony was checking the teacart that his man Dennis had loaded with sandwiches, cakes and hot chocolate for the girls.

Hope had been in many play spaces, but never a converted ballroom and looked about her with wondering approval. She noticed at once that two broad, leather upholstered spanking horses had been angled opposite each other in the center of the room, about eight feet apart.

"For your initiation," Anthony explained.

"How delightful," murmured Hope, alternately eyeing the two exciting men.

"Your fantasy of being dommed by two men at once was interesting to me," said Anthony, "but you never went into the particulars. So I thought we might begin by using Susan as a model." The composer now relieved the surprised Susan of her teacup, took her by the arm and led her over to one of the horses.

"What's this you're doing now?" Susan asked, while being sat upon the horse so that she straddled it.

"I thought it would be fun if Hope were to direct Sloan and I as we visited corporal punishment on you," Anthony explained to his lover, kissing her lightly on the lips. "Then, you see, Sloan and I would know exactly how far she wanted us to go when her own turn came."

"Elegant!" Hope approved, all admiration for her fair-haired associate, clad to perfection in a smoky blue velvet princess cut dress that buttoned down the front and revealed at collar, sleeves and hem cream frills of stiff lawn. When the skirt was pulled up, the framing of panties and petticoat around pink and white skin evoked the tints and tones of the high Renaissance. "My surrogate is exquisitely lovely, but I'm sure she deserves to be spanked and strapped and caned!" Hope declared. Sloan found the toy chest and made some selections.

Knowing that whatever she told them to do to Susan would soon be done to herself, Hope was careful in her instructions. Mostly she wanted to see Susan's divine bottom punished by one man, while the other held her fast, pinched her ear lobes, unbuttoned her dress to expose and firmly squeeze her cherry tipped bosom, caress her throat, wind his hand in her long, blonde hair and quite often, spread her bottom cheeks to afford the other man access to her tiny anus and dewy vagina. Hope couldn't help but dwelling on these areas and begging both Anthony and Sloan take turns spanking and whipping them with a small, light flogger. Susan bore all of these attentions with the soft passivity common to all submissives that are getting what they want. Though none of them mentioned it, all noticed that Susan climaxed after fifty or sixty firm taps of a riding crop directly on her bottom hole while being held fast to the horse. But all of them knew that now it was Hope's turn to be disciplined and Susan's turn to watch.

David was smoking, drinking coffee, grading essays and musing on his first mash note of the semester when Hope arrived home amid a fanfare of lightning and thunder.

"Darling, guess what I've been doing?" Hope sat down and told him all. David stopped grading essays but continued to smoke. Finally he extended his palm and said, "Give." For a moment she did not understand. "Come on," he snapped his fingers. Transfixed by his cool, narrow gaze, Hope placed seven hundred dollar bills in his hand. "Is that it?"

"Yes."

"You let a millionaire pay you seven for all that?" David pushed back his chair, pulled her across his lap and smacked her hard across the back of her pleated skirt twelve or thirteen times. "Hereafter I'll expect you to drive a harder bargain," he instructed, setting her back on her feet. Then David slipped the cash into his billfold and went back to grading his essays. "Now, suppose you get me dinner," he ordered, fixing her with a very stern gaze. Hope hugged him hard before running to perform this beloved task.

Chapter Four

Spring Rain

As four o'clock struck on the first Friday afternoon in April, David Lawrence exited his office, briefcase in hand. Pausing before the frosted glass door of his neighbor, Paula Rohan, he drew a sheet of paper from his breast pocket, scanned it for the twentieth time, folded it back up and knocked.

The comely guidance counselor invited him in. She was seated behind her large desk, a daintily voluptuous blonde of thirty, with the complexion of a shepherdess-Venus from 17th Century oil. In her divinely feminine presence, David's pulse began to quicken.

"Oh, hello David," Paula trilled, loading her expensive leather satchel with all manner of things. "Feel free," she pushed an ashtray toward him as he took a seat opposite her.

"Thanks. Paula, I need some advice."

"From me?"

"One of the girls has sent me a mash note and I don't know how to respond."

"Well, how do you normally respond?" Paula leaned forward to light his cigarette with a heavy marble lighter that one of the pupils had given her for Christmas.

"Thanks. How do you know it's happened before?" He pulled out the note. Paula smiled, for David Lawrence was a male she was greatly disposed to admire. "I never know how to respond," he admitted. "So I was wondering whether the school had a policy on such matters."

"May I see?" Paula extended one perfectly manicured, be-ringed and braceleted hand for the letter. David gave it to her and she read it aloud.

"*To Mr. Lawrence,*

> *As you in the classroom stand*
> *I fixate on your slender hand*
> *Winding in my long, black hair*
> *Stripping me completely bare–*"

Paula raised her periwinkle eyes. "This is pretty hot stuff."
"It gets better," he replied.
She continued reading,

"*As your dulcet tones reveal*
What makes Captain Ahab feel
What makes John the Savage weep
And old Goriot so cheap–
In my Powerbook I note
Why upon your face I dote
Why your voice gives me a thrill
Why you leave me with no will.
No Raskolinov am I
To cause anyone to die
Would it matter quite so much
If your lithe form I did touch?
I would wear a letter red
If you'd let me give you head–
Memorize Eugene Onegin
If you'd treat me like a pagan
Don wool jammies with a flap
But to grind upon your lap."

Paula paused to grin at David then continued reading,

"*Gertrude was wanton in Hamlet*
I truly long to be your pet

Lysastrada bartered sex
(My pedigree is double X)
With just three months left to the year
I must make myself clear
Please grant the boon I crave
And let me be your slave.

Please email your response to:
lupefreeman@mindspring.com"

"My," said Miss Rohan, handing the page back to David with reverence. "Did she manage to reference every book you assigned this semester?"

"Uh huh."

"Lupe Freeman, eh?" Paula called up the student's record on her computer. "Oh, delightful!" Paula clapped her hands, "You must have been born under a lucky star."

"Why? What do you see?"

"Lupe Freeman turns eighteen tomorrow."

"That's great, but there's still the question of how to react. The last time this happened I simply stopped talking to the girl until after graduation. Do you think that I should do the same thing here?"

"Why bother?" Paula shrugged.

"Well, because of the delicacy of the situation. She's my student after all. I imagine Braemar expects impeccable etiquette from the male instructors."

"Ha, Mr. Lawrence. If they cared about anything like that they wouldn't hire teachers who look like movie stars."

"Paula, don't tease. This is serious."

"Is it?"

"Well, isn't it?"

"David, were you aware that Braemar is the school where kids go when they've been thrown out of every other prep school in New England?"

"I find that hard to believe. These kids are the best students I've ever taught."

"I didn't say they got thrown out of the other schools for academic reasons, did I?"

"Then what are you talking about?"

"Haven't you ever heard of sex and drugs? And haven't you yet figured out that Braemar is a party school?"

"Actually, no."

"That's good. Project an air of innocence always. It becomes you. But understand that our sole job here is to get every kid at Braemar into an ivy league college. For that the parents are paying us 60 K a year per delinquent. How do we manage to make these spoiled brats of millionaire hippies cram for exams and spend their weekends on campus when they've fled from every other boarding school they've ever been interred in?"

"Cute uniforms?"

"That helps, but mainly it's the coed dorms."

"The parents go for that?"

"Well, let's take Lupe Freeman's for example." Paula consulted her screen. "Lupe's mom is a punk vocalist and sexual performance artist from L.A. named Saturnia X."

"Saturnia X!" cried David; "I used to follow her band in the 80's."

"Guess what Lupe's dad does?"

"I can't imagine."

"He's Ron Freeman, notorious publisher of men's magazines, champion of free speech and unrepentant icon of sexual vulgarity since you and I were in high school."

"So that's what she meant about the double X lineage."

"So, want to try writing home a note of complaint to mom and dad because their early admissions to Vassar, legally adult daughter happened to write you a poem?"

'I don't guess they'd have much sympathy."

"And I'm sure you don't expect Braemar to offend or upset Lupe by asking her to stop pestering you. Remember, we need everyone of those sixty G's Mr. Freeman is paying us for her senior year."

"I see your point, though it is rather a different way of looking at things than I'm used to."

"So you see, you must handle the Lupe situation yourself and not trouble her parents. Or the school. After all, you don't want the administration to think you aren't up to the first simple problem that arises."

"What do you suggest?"

"Well, you might invite the class to your home for tea, thus exposing Lupe to her rival, your beautiful wife."

"Except then she'd know where I live."

"True."

"Anything else? I mean, ought I to confront her pointblank?"

"Why not?"

"Which response do you think would make her like me less: a gentle rejection or a good scolding?"

"Only time and distance will make her like you less."

"Thanks, you helped a lot," said David, rising.

"Oh, you're welcome. And remember, if all else fails, paddling is still an option."

"Is that so?" he lingered in the door, smiling at her irreverence.

"Of course!"

"What do you mean?"

"It's in every student contract that all the parents sign."

"You're kidding."

"No."

"Maybe thirty years ago."

"Maybe thirty days ago," she corrected him. "How else do you think our cute, young female teachers repel passes from the boys?"

David looked at her hard and saw that she was teasing him again.

"Better be careful, Miss Rohan, if paddling really is an option."

David noted the blush that spread over her flawless complexion as she slipped on a cardigan, picked up her purse and preceded him out of her office.

"Need a lift?" she asked, remembering that David's wife had dropped him off that morning.

"Is Pigeon Cove on your way?"

"Completely."

A few minutes later he was seated beside her in a luxury sedan. He noticed she was still faintly blushing.

"Why aren't you married, Paula?" he boldly asked.

"I haven't got the body type men like."

"Silly. You're stunning."

Paula looked at him.

"You think so?"

"I was just thinking today how classic your beauty is."

"And one might call you a connoisseur," she smiled.

"Oh, because of Hope? Getting her was just dumb luck, believe me."

"I'll be she wraps you around her little finger."

"On the contrary. I'm always careful to maintain the upper hand."

"How do you manage that?"

"As you said, paddling is always an option," he replied, getting out of the car when she came to a stop in front of Cobweb Cottage. "Come in for coffee?"

"Is Hope at home?"

"She's at work until six-fifteen."

"Then I don't dare come in."

"Why not?"

"I just don't trust myself," she answered truthfully, thrilled to think that he might not have been kidding about paddling his wife.

"Okay wise guy, be like that," David bid her good-bye and watched her drive away.

Lupe Freeman had been summoned to David's office. She arrived, all atremble, a slight girl with good skin and straight black hair to her waist. She wore her summer uniform of a grey cotton skirt, vest and white blouse. Size 5 black Italian loafers adorned her feet and hose her shapely legs, as became a senior. In contrast to her epistolary cheekiness, David found her present demeanor endearing meek, which ironically caused him to jettison his rehearsed speech of sensitive rejection and instead sternly order her to sit down.

Dropping into his own chair he lit a cigarette and pushed her poem across the desk. "How dare you send me such an impertinent letter?" Shocked by his severity and speechless with shame Lupe rose to flee.

"Sit, I said." She obeyed him as a lump rose in her throat. "Miss

Freeman, what were you thinking when you know that I'm a married man?"

Lupe pressed her hand to her face in the melodramatic style of a silent film star, reminding David of the gesture he had seen her mother use many times on stage at The Roxy. "Oh Lupe," he suddenly said, in a quite normal tone, "I used to follow Saturnia X fifteen years ago."

This friendly admission dispelled much of her anxiety and Lupe subsided in the chair. "Oh. How nice."

"At any rate, young lady, we can't have any more of this," he indicated the poem.

"No," she agreed, the color coming and going in her olive complected face.

"And at the moment I don't need a slave," he added, tossing her a look that made her tummy contract. "However, I could use a research assistant. Are you available?"

"Yes!" Joy lit Lupe's brown eyes.

"Okay," he replied dismissively.

"Mr. Lawrence?"

"Well?"

"I never meant to offend you."

"I understand."

"Usually older men are flattered when I write them a poem."

"Oh, you do this often, do you?" he bristled.

"Mr. Lawrence?"

"Yes, Miss Freeman?"

"Do you think there's a possibility that we could ever have sex?"

"I think there's a possibility that I could turn you over my knee," he warned her.

"That would be a first," she murmured.

"I'll bet it would."

"A spanking seems very erotic," she observed.

"You would know a thing like that," he sighed.

The following Sunday afternoon David and Hope had the senior lit class over to a cookout on the beach. The weather was unseasonably warm and in her crisp white shorts and halter top, with her flat midriff exposed and her long blonde hair unrestrained, Hope made a fabulous impression. Lupe was beguiled by the consort of her idol and talked to her nearly the whole afternoon. Before the sun went down, Hope was French braiding Lupe's hair.

"I never would have sent that letter if I'd known Mr. Lawrence was married to a babe," Lupe confessed over her shoulder. Hope smiled and placed a tiny kiss on the rim of Lupe's ear.

From that moment on, Lupe transferred half of her affections from her idol to the goddess who empowered him. Lupe and Hope became girlfriends. To David it seemed an excellent resolution to the problem of the crush, which it temporarily was.

Meanwhile, in defiance of all good taste, social and professional etiquette, David had decided that he must have Miss Rohan. Pink, white, perfumed and very nearly sugared, she was too delicious to pass by day after day without craving, though his lust had as much to do with her brain as her luscious contours. Paula was a darling. And so naturally submissive! She seemed made to be dominated by him.

The following Friday afternoon, after classes had let out for the weekend, David took Paula to a late lunch at The Bone and Feather Inn. She had let it slip that her birthday was near and he had fastened on this excuse to ply her with food and wine. Once he'd induced her to drink two glasses, he asked, "Paula dear, do you live alone?"

"Yes, but why?"

"May I see you home?"

"There's no need," she protested.

"You're in no state to drive," he declared. She handed him her car keys. "And besides, I need to give you your birthday spanking."

She occupied the top floor of a Victorian house on Main Street. Lush plants, fresh cut flowers, carved rugs and dramatic window treatments attested to the fact that a woman of substance lived here. In this home of a stylish singleton, without a trace of masculine influence, David breathed a sigh of contentment. He was needed here.

"I wonder if this is proper," she said, appearing with a wine bottle in one hand and corkscrew in the other. "Of course I know it's entirely innocent, but I can't help but wonder what Hope might think."

"It's not entirely innocent and you know it," David said, taking the bottle to open. "And as for Hope, she'll not be the wiser."

"David, how can you? You a newlywed, and with such a wife!" Paula produced glasses, coloring at the turn of conversation.

"I won't deny that Hope has numerous virtues, but sexual fidelity isn't among them. She's already allowed another man to bribe her into accessibility and we've been married less than three months."

"Is that so?" Paula sipped her white wine with fascination.

"Anthony Newton has made her his pet."

"The composer and trustee of Braemar?"

"That's strictly confidential, by the way."

"Poor David."

"It's true," he sighed, "just one man could never satisfy my wife's endless craving for attention."

"How shocking!"

"Yes, I found it so at first, but I'm beginning to see some advantages in the situation for me." They sat on the davenport.

"David, you're making me blush."

"You haven't stopped blushing since we walked in. You must be anticipating the spanking I promised you."

"Nothing of the sort!'

"I like it when you affect primness, Miss Rohan," he said, taking her hand and kissing her palm.

"David, really, you're behaving exactly like a classic wolf!" she protested, pulling her hand away.

"I know. I'm surprised at myself. But you bring it out in me," he admitted, smoothing back her pale blonde pageboy.

"I think you really must be teasing me," she accused, lighting his cigarette.

"Why?"

"Because you have an astonishingly beautiful and by all accounts charming size five wife. Why would you be remotely interested in molesting comfortable size ten me?"

"I think you're lovely and you know it. Besides, you're into it and that makes you irresistible to me."

"It?"

"Spanking, Miss Rohan."

Paula's heart contracted.

"How do you know that?"

"Just from that joke you made the other day about paddlings at Braemar."

"But that was just a joke."

"Sure, but I couldn't help notice the way telling it made you blush. And how you kept blushing all the way home, especially when I mentioned paddling Hope."

"Mr. Lawrence, I'm all aflutter. No one ever guessed my secret before."

"I'm not surprised. There aren't that many of us around. Except in Random Point. There seem to be a lot of us in Random Point for some reason."

Paula watched him crush out his cigarette with a thumping heart. The next thing she knew, he had pulled her across his lap in one swift motion. She didn't dream of resisting.

David couldn't help but guess from the way she caught her breath that this was the first time she had ever been properly turned over a man's knee.

"Now it's time for the counselor to receive some guidance," he informed her before bringing his palm down smartly on her linen skirted seat ten or twelve times. "I don't approve of these self-deprecating remarks I've heard you make about your figure." Another dozen spanks riveted Paula's attention. "I love your figure." To prove it, he spanked her soundly for several minutes. She could do little but whimper and squirm as his hand came relentlessly down.

Many minutes passed as he spanked her on her skirt, the action bringing back his own innocently perverse high school days, when he would persuade girlfriends to take protracted spankings across his lap. High school girls were so sweetly compliant.

Then had come nearly two sober decades of politically activated mates, all rabidly opposed to being turned over his knee. Periodically haunting pick-up bars he had once or twice turned up women drunk enough to not care whether he spanked them or not, but he was not cynical enough to pursue this hobby with any degree of commitment.

Finally he had had discovered the professional B&D scene, which alone could guarantee him a supply of girls to spank. Of course he had to pay for this privilege, but at that point it hardly seemed to matter, so keen was his frustration with never being able to spank a pretty woman. Luckily his adventures in the dungeon began and ended with Hope, the most popular professional submissive in Hollywood, with whom he began living out his fantasies on a weekly basis. The vice was expensive but ever so satisfying, especially as Hope soon fell in love with him and quit working in a dungeon to become his girlfriend.

The marriage was a whimsical notion of David's, hatched in Hollywood a few days before their departure for Massachusetts, when he still imagined Braemar to be a rigidly strict boarding school with Victorian standards of propriety.

David adored Hope and she him. But so habituated was she to playing with a variety of partners, that David quickly realized theirs would be an open marriage. Therefore he had decided to adapt and that meant seizing opportunities like this golden one.

Pulling up her skirt to reveal a pure silk slip, garter belt, panties and seamed stockings, David paid due homage to Paula's round bottom and white thighs with the palm of his hand.

"I'm not even going to pull your panties down this time," he told her, pulling them aside however to examine her reddened cheeks. A tangible heat rose from her luminous skin. He massaged her deeply, for he had been spanking her quite hard for at least twenty-five minutes. Her complexion was fair and she was so unused to spanking that he feared to mark her. Yet spanking her was hypnotically seductive. She seemed content to lie across his lap for as long as he chose to keep her there.

Finally he pulled her up and gathered her into his arms. She hid her face, still vibrating with pleasure. "Will you forgive me for taking advantage of you?" he asked.

"I forgive you, I thank you and I think I love you," she replied, hugging him hard.

David became Paula's disciplinarian. They met in the afternoons several times a week. Since Hope never got home before six-fifteen, he felt virtually safe from detection. But as smart as he was, he couldn't think of everything.

Lupe had noted the change in David and Paula and continued observation brought her knowledge, disappointment and distress. Lupe was outraged that Mr. Lawrence, whom she had so revered and lusted after, could be caught in the toils of a pearl and cashmere wearing, sugar-fed cream tart like Miss Rohan when Hope in all her sleek and tapered youth was not only available to gratify his every erotic desire, but also cheerfully brought home a pay check, cooked and cleaned! Furious with her ex-idol's inconstancy, Lupe went to his goddess consort with the story.

Naturally Hope reeled. Of course she knew that this was happening because she'd played with Anthony Newton. Possibly David had also found out about her letting Hugo Sands cane and birch her. Hope bit her knuckle with anxiety. Miss Rohan was lovely and witty. And her office was right next to his.

Hope was madly jealous. How dare he marry her and make love to a sweater girl two months later?

"My husband is having an affair," Hope announced to Sloan, at five p.m. that afternoon, "may I go home and brood?"

"You shouldn't believe everything you hear," Sloan scolded gently, using his pristine handkerchief to blot the two tears that had rolled down Hope's cheeks. "Give David a chance to explain before you despair."

"May I appropriate that?" she took the handkerchief and made good use of it on the way home.

Her initial impulse on arriving home was to simply drop into a chair and sob her heart out. But a glance at her eyes in the mirror told her that she'd already done enough crying for one day. As angry as she was at her husband, she still wanted to make a good impression when he arrived home.

Choosing an outfit was a soothing exercise. She finally decided on a navy cotton apron dress that clung to each slim curve and revealed a fair amount of bare thigh. Navy clogs displayed her pink heels with insouciance and her mouth was a full crimson pout.

Now on this of all days David was late in arriving home. Noticing the answering machine flickering for the first time, Hope punched it on. "Hi honey. I'm staying a little later tonight to write up some college referrals. If you get this message come by and pick me up at around seven."

That was encouraging anyway. The normal tone of David's voice and request had a calming effect on the bride. Even though it was only six, Hope got into the car and headed for Braemar.

On the way her heart ached with the thought that they might be in a tête-à-tête when she rapped on the door. "Pull yourself together!" she exhorted her reflection in the rear view mirror. "Show dignity, composure, inner strength!" Oh, the deceit of the man!

Faintly disappointed at the emptiness of the corridor, and the absence of Miss Rohan, Hope pushed open David's door and marched in, her arms crossed on her chest. He looked up from his desk and smiled. "Hello darling! Don't you look yummy? You're early but as it turns out I'm just about done." He quickly saved his work and turned from his computer to greet her properly. "Let's go out tonight! "

She suffered herself to be kissed then petulantly put five or six feet between them.

"Hope, what's the matter?"

"I'll tell you when we get out of here."

Once they were in the car, with David behind the wheel he waited for her to speak.

"Aren't you going to start the motor?"

"Tell me what's going on."

"I know about you and Miss Rohan."

David started the car and they drove off the Braemar grounds. "What do you know?"

"That you've been having an affair." Hope's arms were folded again and her eyes clouded with tears.

"Who told you that?"

"Lupe."

"Well she's misinformed."

"You're not having an affair with Miss Rohan?"

"No."

"No?"

"Not as such."

"What does that mean?"

"We've never had sex."

"Oh. Really?"

"I can't believe Lupe said that."

"She must have had a reason."

"Oh, I've seen Miss Rohan all right."

"Seen her! What exactly does that mean?"

"It means that Miss Rohan has no one to spank her so I've been accommodating her."

"What's this you're saying now? Miss Rohan's in the Scene? You see her to play?"

"Exactly," David said, pulling up to the Bone and Feather Inn.

Hope was somewhat placated by David's explanation, but continued to brood.

"So, why doesn't she find herself a Scene boyfriend? Hugo's personal ads magazine is teeming with eligible bachelors."

"I never thought of that. I'll bring her a copy tomorrow," David said agreeably.

"She has no right coming on to another girl's husband!" Hope declared, on her second glass of wine.

"She didn't come onto me."

"Does that mean that you came on to her?"

David shrugged.

"You certainly got bored of me quickly!"

"Hope, it's not like that."

"Well, what is it like?"

"Drink more wine while I make it clear."

"Poor, dear Miss Rohan," Hope almost sobbed into her architectural dessert one and one half glasses later. "Never got to play for thirty whole years!"

"The thing that gets me is Lupe Freeman's insolence at running to you with this dangerous rumor!" David hit the tabletop with his fist, bringing the innkeeper Connie running with a second bottle.

"It's just because she doesn't want to see me wronged," Hope pointed out, lighting her husband's cigarette with a feeling of infinite well-being. To think that one's husband was having an affair and then find out that he was only occasionally spanking a pleasant lady five years older and twenty pounds heavier than one was a fine thing.

"It's awkward though. I hardly want Lupe to know the truth about my relationship with Miss Rohan."

"That's true. The whole school would know that you and Miss Rohan are spanking enthusiasts in a couple of days."

"I don't think that would go down, even at Braemar."

"Too bad you and Miss Rohan were so obvious."

David's chin went up.

"You just had to be a slut and play at work," Hope continued to needle.

"Force of habit," he admitted.

"Never fear, darling. Lupe need never learn the truth."

"She's sure to ask about what happened when you confronted me."

"Silly, you don't imagine that I took her seriously when she told me about you and Miss Rohan? Just the opposite. I told her I was sure she was mistaken."

"Really?"

"Well, I remembered that you and Miss Rohan are on the prom committee and suggested that you'd probably been meeting because of it."

"Hope, I'm speechless."

"That's something new."

"Bless your quick little brain."

"Don't mention it."

David, finishing his fourth glass of wine, began to feel almost worshipful of his wife and deeply sighed.

"What?"

"You're sweet," he said, kissing her hand and then behind her ear. "But it makes me sad."

"What makes you sad, silly?"

"This sudden burst of maturity."

"Surely you've notice prior to this that I am a rational creature?"

"Not entirely. Tsk. It's very sad," David mused with his chin on his hand.

"What on earth is sad, dearest?"

"That I'll never feel able to discipline you again."

"What?" she cried.

"It's true," he lamented, crushing out his cigarette and rising to leave. "You're no longer suitable for spanking."

"David, what the hell are you babbling about?" She followed him out to the street where they got in their car and began the short drive home to Cobweb Cottage through a light mist.

"Somehow, you've grown up," he insisted, weaving ever so slightly along the slick, narrow coast road.

"Oh, David, I'll never be too grown up for corporal punishment," she assured him, squeezing his arm and nuzzling his cheek.

"You are right now," he emphatically stated, thumping the wheel. "I mean, dear, just look at how reasonably you handled my sordid confession. You were a perfect angel."

"Actually, it was rather a clean confession."

"Say what you will, you won't change my mind," he predicted as they debarked on Pigeon Cove and walked into their bungalow.

"David, you're drunk and not fit to discuss such an important topic!" she snapped, then suddenly stricken with a sobering thought, Hope murmured more gently, "David, you're not choosing this precise moment to come out as a switch, are you?"

David smiled and shook his head. "No."

"Well, that's something anyway."

"Miss Rohan is very dear," David explained with the maudlin sentimentality of advanced inebriation. "I'm the first one who ever spanked her since her father. You should see how she looks up to me."

"But I look up to you. I always have."

David sighed. "Perhaps intellectually. But it's always hard spanking you. Right from the start at The Keep, you were the experienced one, teaching me how to use the equipment, honing my technique. I could only just barely feel superior to you back then because you were such a wayward child. But you've become responsible lately!"

"Oh bunk! You're in your cups and talking rot." Hope opened the windows to let in the sea air and sound of the cove.

"There's truth in the grape," he replied.

Hope had changed into a white dressing gown and was brushing out her long corn silk hair at the vanity when he entered their bedroom.

"Come to bed, darling," he patted the pillows.

"I think not," she returned, laying down the brush.

"Not tired?"

"Exhausted and dejected, but I'd rather breakfast on organ meats than share a bed with you tonight, you quitter!"

"But why? Because I respect you more tonight than I've ever done before?"

"You think just because I've played a good deal that I'm not innocent!"

"Of course you're not innocent."

"Well, I'm not jaded either. My tummy still contracts when I'm put across the right man's lap. That makes me just as tender and deserving as Miss Rohan! And by the way, if it was always so hard to spank me at The Keep why did you pay to see me twenty-four times in a row?"

"Love."

"I see, love made the horrid ordeal of spanking me possible."

"Hope, you're an ideal playmate, but naturally you could never seem as submissive to me as a girl who'd never been dominated before."

"Oh, go to hell. I violently hate and will be leaving you first thing in the morning."

"Hope, come to bed."

"Make me," she cried, throwing the hairbrush at his head. Deftly ducking the missile he came across the room and tried to take her in his arms.

"Don't you dare try to kiss me, you adulterer!" She pushed him away and dealt him a ringing slap across the face.

"Why, you little brat!" He took her by the shoulders and gave her a shake. She laughed, remembering how much he disliked being slapped. The last time she tried it she'd gotten six of the best and sodomized.

"Well?" she demanded, slapping him again, even harder. The next thing she knew he dragged her over to the bed, turned her over his knee and spanked her.

"Thank you for waking me up," he said between hard smacks. "I forgot for one split second how impossible you are!"

Again and again his hard hand came down upon her robed seat.

"Ouch!" she periodically whimpered as David's palm relentlessly descended. Hope could not recall ever honing David's technique, but his serious demeanor continued to give her butterflies one full year after he had taken her across his lap for the first time. "Oooooh!" she exhaled when he occasionally paused in the punishment to stroke and massage her slim, oval cheeks.

Pulling up the dressing down to expose her pinkened bottom was David's next occupation.

"I will not receive a bare bottom spanking from an unrepentant adulterer!" Hope protested, wriggling.

"I did not commit adultery."

"You fell in love, which is worse!"

"Silly."

"She's virtually alienated your affections!"

"It's really not that way."

Several harder whacks followed. She panted and squirmed. "Let me go!"

"I will not."

"You said you wouldn't spank me."

"Apparently I've changed my mind."

Her white skin was already tinged dark pink from his hand. Now each fresh slap brought up a darker red.

"Ow! That's beginning to really sting! Stop, I tell you, David. It's sore!"

"Beg my pardon for slapping my face."

"No!"

"Fine, you can do it while you're being fucked and dildo-fucked." David summarily put her off his lap.

"No!" she protested again, though weakly as he routed through the linen chest for Hope's compact cache of sex toys. "This is no time for polymorphous perversity," she objected, hiding her face in the pillows while disposing her body in a deliberately accessible manner.

"Oh yes it is. You need it," he assured her, choosing a dildo for her bottom.

Sitting up against the headboard, David made Hope straddle his lap facing him and take his large, throbbing erection in her pussy to the root. This operation complete, he bared her bottom for his hand and continued with the spanking until she was grinding against him. The anal plug was inserted and holding it in place with one hand, David spanked her with the other.

"No!" she protested at each stage of the humiliating exercise, but ever more faintly, burying her face in his shoulder.

"Beg my pardon," he insisted, fucking and dildoing her with deep strokes.

"I do," she agreed, and succumbed to a climax that for once didn't find her face down. He prolonged her tremors by biting her shoulders and throat while murmuring endearments and praise.

A little later, as they lay listening to the surf, Hope curled against him. "So we'll find Miss Rohan a boyfriend, right?" she asked, with her husband's hand pressed to her lips.

"I'll leave it in your hands," he assented, blithely breathing in the scent of her hair.

"You really scared me for a second there," she protested, unaware that he had fallen fast asleep.

At around six on the following rainy Monday Lupe Freeman entered David's office without knocking. He looked up from grading reports.

"There's the background on the authors you wanted me to research," she announced, tossing a disc onto his desk, extracting a cigarette from his pack and lighting it with a box match. Surprised but not astonished, David waited for her to speak. She sat in the window seat and examined the darkening sky. "I told Hope about you and the roly-poly pudding, but she didn't believe me."

"I beg your pardon?"

"I ratted you out about Miss Rohan."

"Is that so?"

"I guess I feel a little bit guilty about it, but since Hope didn't believe me, I suppose there's no harm done," Lupe reflected. David folded his arms to keep from throttling her. "Except that now you hate me worse than before," she added, finally meeting his eyes. "If only you'd given me sex when I'd asked you for it I wouldn't have been so jealous of you and Miss Rohan," she sighed.

"Oh, we're back to that, are we?"

"If you can get it up for Cuddles, why not me?"

"Miss Freeman, I'll thank you not to be so familiar."

"Mr. Lawrence, are you really indifferent to me or just pretending to be indifferent because I'm your student? Because if it's the latter you should know that half the seniors here are sleeping with their teachers."

"That rumor is probably as true as the one you've been spreading about me and Miss Rohan."

"Ask Miss Rohan. She knows all our secrets."

"And you know none of hers."

"Can you deny that you love her?" Lupe shrewdly demanded, causing her teacher to color.

"What a little termagant you are," David mildly declared, loading his briefcase with materials.

"I don't mean to be. It's just that I'm so insanely smitten with you."

"Look me up ten years from now. If you still feel the same way, we'll talk."

"In ten years you'll be doddering! The way you smoke you'll be dead. We'd better not waste another moment."

David smiled.

"Just lock the door and bend me over the desk," she tempted him. "See, I'm even wearing a skirt. It would be so easy."

"If I bend you over the desk, young lady, it will be to cane you."

"Okay!"

"Lupe, get out of here. Now."

"No. I want to be caned by you."

"I wonder if I could get fired for caning you?"

"No way in hell, Mr. Lawrence."

"In that case, Miss Freeman, you've got until you finish that cigarette to enjoy the act of sitting."

David locked the door, pulled the blinds and reached into his desk for a neat little school cane he'd obtained at Hugo Sands' antique shop. Next he took Lupe by the forearm and bent her over his desk, marking her sudden gasp with great interest.

"Miss Freeman, you assume the position like a natural," he commented, noticing her arch her back and straighten her legs. She'd chosen to wear her winter uniform that chilly April day, with its becoming black and white pleated plaid skirt, black vest and white blouse. Her high-heeled saddle shoes passed Braemar muster in that they didn't clash with any thing else she had on. The anklets were pure white in contrast to her olive-toned bare legs.

"My boyfriend sophomore year used to whip me frequently," she confided over one shoulder. "He was a bi-leatherman and a fabulous top."

"Oh! That explains a lot."

"But I've never had a caning before. That's what I like about older men, they always know the most perverted ways to give a girl thrills."

"You're not here for thrills, Miss Freeman. You're here for discipline." David tapped the cane against the palm of his hand. Then he snorted, "So your ex is a bi leather top, eh? You sound safe as houses."

"Oh, we never had sex. He said I was too young. He only whipped and tied me up. I adored him."

"Aren't you the little sophisticate?"

"Don't you think most girls my age are aware of B&D?"

"Maybe in Hollywood."

"I'm from Hollywood."

"Well, I don't suppose we can put off this disagreeable duty any longer," David sighed, positioning the cane across her bottom. "Just remember, young lady, you brought this entirely on yourself."

"I will. Thank you."

"Lupe, you're wriggling and fidgeting. Hold still or I won't be able to aim properly."

Folding back her short skirt David revealed her small sized but perfectly well rounded bottom, snugly encased in pristine white cotton panties. Pausing a moment to pay this sacred image the reverence it deserved, he tested the cane against the palm of his hand.

"Lupe, this may sting, but mindful of where we are, I want a minimum of noise out of you. Understand?"

"Everyone's out of this part of the building. I checked." She pillowed her chin on her hands and closed her eyes.

With a swish of the cane David carefully placed the first stroke across the centermost portion of her slim buttocks. In the larger world of caning, it was no more than a flirtatious tap, but it made Lupe catch her breath and shift on her feet, bending her knees momentarily.

"Hold your position, I said."

"I will."

The next stroke landed directly below the first and just as juicily. She made a tiny murmur but did not shift this time. The cane left a faint horizontal dent across the white cotton mounds of her bottom. He kept one hand in the small of her back and carefully aimed to administer parallel strokes, one below the other for three, then back up again for three more.

"Getting bored?"

"No, sir!"

"It's best to ease into a caning, I've found. Forgive me, Miss Freeman, but perfect as these are, it's necessary they come down," he said, tugging her panties down to mid-thigh to entirely expose her. Unembarrassed she waited breathlessly.

Swish! A crisp stroke fell. A small cry then broke from her lips.

"Remember, Lupe, no noise."

David began to apply measured strokes, letting each sink in before giving the next. Light pink lines formed against her olive-hued skin where his cane neatly struck. Lupe whimpered in their wake but arched her bottom higher. She acknowledged that her teacher could be charmingly strict. Looking back she thrilled to the concentration wrinkling his brow. He noticed her looking at him and narrowed his eyes at her. She quickly turned frontwards again.

"You have such a tiny bottom that I have to aim just right," he complained, punishing her with swats that made her flinch. Now approaching the realm of real caning, each stoke not only stung her silky surface skin but resonated deep into her firm, muscular flesh. A recovery time of a moment or two was allowed between strokes, during which it took immense will power for David to abstain from tenderly smoothing her reddening backside.

"I suppose you prefer the ample seat of that battledore next door."

"Lupe, that's the third cruel epithet you've flung at my comely associate since entering this office." David now redressed these insults to Miss Rohan with the hardest stroke so far. It made Lupe straighten up and clutch her bottom with a yip. "Shall we continue?" He pushed her back down over the desk.

Lupe rebelliously kicked off her panties and assumed the position with her legs astraddle rather than modestly together as before. Her adorable sex she thrust towards him in the most alluring way. "Unfair of you to flaunt your charms like that at a married man," he admonished, administering another stern stroke. She rocked with it but held her position, dewy with excitement. Not touching her was a bit of self-imposed discipline which David felt a necessary counterbalance to all the other rules he was breaking.

"I was wondering when you'd make me a compliment."

"This entire interview is a compliment, my dear."

However, his resolve began to crumble when it occurred to him to tease her with the cane between her legs. This allowed him to touch her discreetly without using his hands. When he stopped the cane came away wet. And she seemed on the verge of a climax.

Suddenly Lupe's beauty and accessibility, combined with her superb reaction to the caning made her impossible to resist. He turned her around to face and him and took her by the shoulders. "If this can stay our secret I'll get you off," he promised firmly.

"I wouldn't tell under torture," she instantly replied, having never kept a secret in her life.

"In that case," he let the phrase trail off, took her by the hand and led her to the small leather sofa. Sitting down he pulled her down across his lap.

"Are you going to spank me?"

"That would make too much noise," he said regretfully, pulling up her skirt to expose her again. "But I thought you might like the positioning." Spreading her legs and dividing her coral labia with nimble fingers, David exposed her with the excitement of a user unwrapping a drug. He could no longer refrain from plunging a middle finger up into her creamy, clinging recesses. Lupe made a soft but gratifying noise and immediately ground against his lap. One more finger invaded her pussy while with the other hand he squeezed and separated her cheeks.

"Oh please!" she cried.

"What do you want?"

"I can't say it," she confessed.

"Oh!" David began to lightly spank then deeply masturbate her tiny anus. In two minutes Lupe came hard. Her shudders told the story. David pulled her skirt back down and made her sit up. He resisted the impulse to take her in his arms and hug her, feeling somehow that Hope wouldn't like that. But he did brush a tendril of hair off her face and straighten her collar.

"Miss Freeman, you are dismissed."

Chapter Five

Not So Fast!

Hope took the problem of finding a boyfriend for Miss Rohan to Hugo Sands.

The interview took place in the office of Hugo's fine antiques shop, where he gave Hope tea and treats several afternoons a week. Late April showers were flooding the cobble stoned streets of Random Point and few patrons were tinkling store bells as his comely visitor watched the spanking magazine publisher step through his data base in search of an unexceptionable bachelor to satisfy Miss Rohan's needs.

"You've only been married two months and David's already having an affair? I thought I was bad," Hugo commented.

"It's more like an innocent spanking relationship to hear my beloved tell it, but I'm sure I'll feel uneasy until the young lady's affections are otherwise engaged."

"What's this husband stealer like?"

"Oh, she's adorable. Just turned 30, ivy educated, natural blonde, peach complexion, slightly voluptuous, superb taste, exquisitely feminine and very submissive."

"If all of that is true then Ambrose Bartlett might be a possibility," said Hugo, perusing a friend's customer record.

"I love the name."

"If he goes for Miss Rohan it might be a good thing for her."

"Why so?"

"He owns Bartlett's Department store in Woodbridge. Know it?"

"Yes, the only store on the Cape that stocks Fogal stockings. What's he like, Hugo?"

"Early 40's, sophisticated, meticulous and very domineering. Runs the store like Von Stroheim."

"Tell me more."

"He's jaded. He's been playing in the scene for about fifteen years and claims he's never met a submissive with a brain. He's also prefers your body type as I recall. Just how voluptuous is Miss Rohan?"

"Seven to ten pounds away from being a Marilyn."

"H'm. Could we put her on a diet before their first date?"

"Don't be silly! This girl is a babydoll. Remember, she's distracted David from me. Plus she's got that brain Mr. Bartlett has been looking for and is practically a Scene virgin. How could the old roué resist?"

"He might find it more convenient to engage the professional services of our local movie star," Hugo smiled and gave her a pat on her brand new dark blue jeans. Hope had been featured in a number of esoteric films before departing from the coast the previous winter and a collector like Ambrose would own them all. Hugo always liked to expose deserving submissives to men who might be inclined to patronize them.

"Is he cute?"

"Not bad. About 6'2" and trim with a pencil moustache. I'm sure you'd find him generous."

"Does he come to your parties? I'd play with him for free at a party."

"Ambrose Bartlett doesn't waste time on polite spanking parties. He likes to get a woman entirely alone and become quite intimate with her at once."

"Who doesn't? But I hope he doesn't expect to do everything on the first night! Miss Rohan is a lady."

"I didn't know they still made those."

"David says she even wears full slips."

"That might intrigue Ambrose, then again, it might remind him of his mother. Do ladies allow themselves to be manually manipulated on a first date?"

"Of course. Look, book him with Miss Rohan first and reserve me for afters. Maybe he'll be so taken with Miss Rohan that he won't need to see me after all."

"Or do you want to search further?" Hugo began stepping through his database again, wondering whether Miss Rohan might be too refined for his worldly friend.

"No! Paula deserves her chance at a man who owns a good department store."

Paula was humiliated when David revealed Hope and Hugo's plans for her future happiness. But she realized they were right. Her innocently illicit relationship with a married man was all too quickly turning her heart inside out. That the man's wife was responding with the height of courtesy demanded equal respect on Paula's side. That could only be demonstrated by transferring her honest affections to an unattached dominant male. Now that she knew that such creatures existed, it was time to find one of her own.

Through worrying, being in love and looking forward to regular spankings from David, Paula had lost weight and could no longer be accurately described as voluptuous. This phenomenon had occurred unbeknownst to Hope, who had only met Paula once at the beginning of the semester. David had not bothered to tell his wife that his playmate was growing more delectable by the moment and this was how the initial confusion arose.

Ambrose dined out with Hugo that night and each did their usual amount of drinking. The next morning the department store owner awoke remembering a story about one blonde who needed allowance and another blonde who needed a lover, both of whom had been scheduled by Hugo Sands to meet him that week. As Ambrose understood it, one of the blondes was a sleek ex-B&D player late of Hollywood, now married but still discreetly thrill-seeking in Random Point, while the other was a temptingly buxom guidance counselor employed at The Braemar Academy, newly out in the Scene and seeking a relationship. After calling Hugo to clarify who was who, Ambrose said, "Nix on the plump schoolteacher. I don't have the patience to court a beginner anymore. Send me the beautiful pro though. She'll be handsomely rewarded."

Hugo said, "Fine, she'll meet you at eight," without worrying about the fact that the innocent Miss Rohan was the one he had scheduled for that night's date.

Ambrose Bartlett had no problem mistaking fair and shapely Paula Rohan for slim, blonde Hope Lawrence when Paula walked into the Golden Owl Inn at Woodbridge that night charmingly clad in a size six evening suit that he recognized as a Donna Karan carried at his store.

Ambrose spotted her from the bar and pleasantly went to meet her. She didn't speak much at the outset, affecting shyness but minutely studying him. As he casually ordered the wine she noted how at home he seemed at the Inn and wondered whether all his rendezvous were conducted here. When their waiter retired he pushed an envelope across the table.

"What's that, a card for me?"

"Exactly."

She began to open it.

"No. Put it away for later."

"Oh. Okay." Paula was puzzled by the thickness of the envelope but slipped it into her purse.

"Now tell me exactly what you like," he said when the wine had been poured. "I mean when it comes to playing."

"Oh, we're getting right down to basics, are we?"

"No point in doing anything else, is there?"

"Couldn't we discuss movies and books for a while?"

"Sure. Have you read The Nine and a Half Weeks?"

"Yes. But I only liked the spanking scene."

"I'm not surprised that you like spanking. You have the perfect bottom for it."

"Do you think so?"

"You're blushing."

"I'm not surprised," she pressed her hands to her burning cheeks.

"I expected you to be more blasé," he admitted, topping off their glasses.

"Oh, believe me, I'm finding this very exciting," she admitted, gulping wine for courage. Like most submissives, she preferred the cynical type and Ambrose Bartlett was just remote enough to be thrilling.

"Have we spoken enough about movies and books?" he wondered.

"I suppose so."

"I like the meek and mild stuff. It's very becoming."

"Thank you," she replied guilelessly.

"Pick out what you want for dinner and I'll order it sent up to the suite I've reserved."

Paula consulted the menu. The wine took effect nicely as he rested his chin on his hand and studied her. "How you color, darling," he said mercilessly. "Are you thinking about what I might do to you when I get you alone?"

"I think I'll have the baked salmon," she decided, closing the heavy, tasseled menu gently.

Ambrose ordered dinner and another bottle of wine be sent to the Magistrate's Suite then took Paula upstairs. The inn was very old and without an elevator. Since the short skirt of Paula's blue sharkskin suit displayed her shapely legs and buttocks stunningly, Ambrose insisted she precede him up the winding flight of carpeted stairs to the second floor.

When they reached the landing he noticed that a pout had replaced her smile.

"What's the matter?" he demanded, opening the door to the gracious suite with a key.

"I feel objectified." She walked around the room examining its antique appointments and admiring the marble hearth.

"Well, isn't that your job?" he laughed, coming up behind her as she regarded her reflection in a gilt mirror. He smoothed her perfectly smooth corn silk pageboy down with one hand while the other momentarily squeezed her pert waist.

"My job?" She laughed at the strange remark. The wine arrived and a waiter opened it for them, promising them dinner in a few minutes.

"Did you really mind my looking at your bottom as you walked up the stairs?" Ambrose asked when they were once again alone.

"I'm just surprised that a gentleman would behave that way on such short acquaintance."

Ambrose looked at his companion with dawning comprehension.

"Did I seem like a terrible wolf on the stairs? I'm sorry!" He attempted a quick transition from paying client to well bred escort, now convinced that he had been entirely mistaken in the identity of his guest. This wasn't the pro at all, but the schoolteacher.

She smiled in way of pardon, offering her glass for a refill. He smiled back as he served her, wondering exactly how much wooing would be expected from him before she would agree to let him pull her panties down. The thousands dollars in her purse now guaranteed him absolutely nothing, he realized with a mild surge of resentment. Damn Hugo Sands for ignoring his injunction to send no one to him but the pro. Paula caught him frowning at the thought.

"What were you just thinking?" she asked, sitting on a loveseat by the fire.

"Maybe I'll tell you later."

"Tell me now."

"No."

"Then give me more wine."

"Sure. But don't get so tipsy that you won't want to play."

"Bossy already!"

Dinner arrived before he could retort and took a few minutes to be served. At last the waiter left them alone. Ambrose pulled out her chair briskly and fixed her with a rather cool gaze as he sat opposite her and began lifting covers off plates.

"You are a bossy man, aren't you?"

"Only in that I'm accustomed to giving orders and having them obeyed immediately and without question."

"That's right, I was told that you manage Bartlett's. I scarcely shop anywhere else."

"I thought I recognized that suit."

"I often wondered why it happened to have such an extraordinary hairbrush department. Now I know."

"Did you appreciate the way it's directly adjacent to equestrian accessories?"

"Now that I think of it, that's exactly where I bought my riding crop."

"Good girl."

"Oh, I shop!"

"I'll have to check in my computer and see if you're ever late on your bill."

When a fresh field of pink spread across her fair face Ambrose took note. He refilled her glass cunningly and waited for one or two more sips to do their work. Already he noticed she was becoming somewhat reckless in her sallies.

"You have been late, haven't you, young lady?"

"Not terribly frequently."

"How frequently?"

"Only occasionally."

"We'll see about that," he promised, pulling a laptop out of the bombe dresser drawer and snapping it open.

"You drag your store around with you on dates?" She got up to look over his shoulder as he accessed his customer records.

"What's your last name?"

"Rohan, Paula."

"Tsk," said Ambrose as a naughty shopping history appeared on the crisp, clear screen. "You're in arrears this very month, Miss Rohan."

"I am?"

"According to this, you've been binge shopping for the last three weeks. Oh! This is very interesting." Ambrose looked at her.

"What?"

"You appear to have dropped two dress sizes over the past four weeks."

"It says that?" Paula's hand went to her throat in shock.

"Naturally the size of every item purchased is entered electronically."

"How horrible!"

"Sit down and finish your dinner," he ordered, "while I decide how to deal with your profligacy." He lit a cigarette and studied her spending history with his store over the last five years.

Paula ate a few more morsels then put down her fork in favor of her wine glass.

"Don't you realize that by missing payments you're incurring 25% interest charges?"

"It's your fault for marking everything up so outrageously."

"Oh, my fault is it? I like that."

Paula walked away from the table with her glass. "Everything in your store is twenty per cent more expensive than it would be at JM's."

"Marble floors and burled armoires don't come free you know."

"You have a point."

"You know, I could wipe out your entire debt to Bartlett's with a keystroke if I choose to do so," Ambrose offered.

"You could?"

"I could. If you comported yourself in a manner that pleased me."

Paula demurely lowered her eyes.

"Of course, you're to be commended for going down two dresses sizes, but a virtue doesn't cancel out a sin. You're unquestionably guilty of over-spending."

While Paula pouted Ambrose wheeled the supper table into the hall, put out the "Do Not Disturb" sign and locked the door.

"Come over here, young lady," he commanded, taking her by the forearm and leading her to a beautifully upholstered bench. "You know where I want you," he told her, pulling her firmly down across his lap.

Ambrose covered the round seat of Paula's snug skirt with smacks that made her squeak and squirm. "This skirt is too tight to be pulled up," he scolded, spanking her harder. "And it will wrinkle if I try to."

"Why not just continue over my skirt?"

Folding back the jacket he noticed that the skirt zipped in back. "Lift up," he ordered, promptly unzipping her skirt. "I'll just pull it off."

Pausing briefly to admire her sheer beige nylon panties and matching, rosetted garter belt, he began to spank her again, bringing his palm down quite firmly on alternate cheeks, until he could observe her flesh turn from cream to pink through the fine beige mesh.

"Ow!" she cried at length. "Don't you believe in rubbing?"

"Not when I mean to be severe."

Paula caught her breath when he pulled her panties down. Then she felt him rub the sting away with deep, circular stokes of his smooth palm. "Mmmm," she murmured, permitting herself to grind ever so lightly against his thighs. "Thank you."

Mesmerized by the beauty of her undulating hips Ambrose put his hand between her thighs to pry them open and found her gloriously wet. "These are only getting in the way," he said, pulling her panties entirely off. "You don't mind, do you?" The spanking recommenced.

"Ow! It hurts much more on the bare!"

"I told you that I meant to be severe."

"But, I'll be good."

"But you've been bad. And you have to be punished for that. Don't you?"

"Isn't the 25% interest punishment enough?"

"Apparently not, as you were back in the store last week using one of your other charge cards." The spanking continued. "I'm going to cut up all your credit cards and put you on an allowance."

"You are?" She turned and smiled at him.

"I've a good mind to take complete control of you."

Paula thought this threat the height of romance. When a tangible heat seemed to rise from her darkly pinkened skin he put her off his lap.

"You can take a break now. Have another drink and pour me one too," he told her, surveying his handiwork as she walked away from him to comply with his orders.

When she returned he stood up and drew her before him to unbutton and remove her hip-length jacket. Her bosom filled her sheer, beige bustier saucily. With her small waist and slightly rounded abdomen, she possessed a torso that no student of classical art could fail to admire. "Lovely," he murmured, turning her around and lightly biting the back of her smooth upper arm. She whimpered at this attention and exposed her throat and shoulders for the same treatment.

"Oooh, do bite me just like that," she sighed, pushing back against him as his arms encircled her waist from behind.

"Sit here and finish your wine while I decided what to do with you next," he ordered at length, making her sit on the upholstered stool. She meekly sipped, now and then rubbing her bottom until he took away her empty glass.

"Straddle the bench, put your hands in front of you and lean forward so your bottom juts out," he instructed, pulling off his suit jacket, loosening his tie, rolling up his sleeves to his elbows and unbuckling his thin leather belt. Paula struck this provocative pose and he took up a position behind her, curling the buckle portion of his belt around his hand to create a proper spanking strap. "Now, young lady, we'll continue."

Paula closed her eyes and waited, her heart contracting with pleasurable apprehension. He snapped the belt once in the air before beginning, then let it fall directly across the plumpest section of her bottom with a sharp report. She made a little noise and shifted on the bench, but held her position. It stung but felt exciting! She was thrilled by her host's expertise. Another lash fell and another. He laid them on firmly and crosswise, from her thighs to her hips and back, up and down in measured strokes, aiming carefully so as not to strike the same place twice in a row. She thrust her bottom out to let him know that all was well and reading her correctly, he began to strap her harder.

Paula whimpered and ground against the bench, eventually dropping her bosom down onto the seat and lowering her palms to the floor in front of her, which protruded and spread her rose-tinted cheeks more dramatically.

Stepping in closer, Ambrose paid her revealed charms the homage they seemed to demand by strapping her lightly vertically, applying the tip of the belt to her anus. When this made her cry, "Oh, God!" and spread her self wider still for his punishing strap he took note. Repeatedly he smacked the tip of the strap against her bottom hole, monitoring her responsive pants.

"You see what a bad girl you are?"

"Yes," she couldn't help but encourage him.

"I suppose you're terribly anal, aren't you, darling?"

"Yes, terribly."

"Do you know you're in a perfect position to have your bottom penetrated?"

Paula answered by shuddering. Ambrose walked away from her and lit a cigarette. "Reach back and spread your bottom for me."

When Paula hesitated he stepped over to her and smacked her hard several times on each cheek. "Do as I tell you."

Paula reluctantly obeyed the embarrassing order.

"Wider. And stay like that. Just like that. It's so perfectly submissive."

Paula whimpered dangerously.

"And don't you dare come," he warned. "At least not yet." Leaving her in this shameful attitude he went into the bedroom to search his overnight bag for a condom. A Rough Rider soon came to hand and he returned to his companion. "All right, you can put your hands back down, but mind you stay just as beautifully open for me."

Coming close to her he dropped to one knee and placing one hand in the small of her back used the other to renew the color in her cheeks. Then he held her open and spanked her anus several dozen times. The sharp smacks went right through her, setting every fiber of her sex a throb. "Naughty! Stop grinding."

"Oh!" She felt deliciously outraged.

"Look at how wet you are," he said, dipping his fingers in her creamy juices and transferring them to her tiny anus. "And just from being punished!"

But when she noticed him open the condom she cried, "Time out, Mr. Bartlett!" and scrambled to her feet.

"What's the matter? Not feeling objectified again, are you?"

"Not exactly, but–"

"But what, dear girl?"

"Well, I never got to have my dessert."

Ambrose gave her a look but went out into the hall to retrieve the ravishing architectural torte and pot of coffee she had requested from the serving cart. When he laid them out on a table for her she had already slipped her panties back on.

"Stalling for time, eh?"

"Uh huh." She took a bite of Belgian chocolate mousse.

"You know if you eat things like that you'll be back up to a size ten before you know it," he warned peevishly.

"H'm. Now you're definitely not going to get sex from me tonight," she decided coolly.

"In that case the debt to the store stands!"

Paula shrugged. "I knew you weren't serious about that anyway."

"Certainly I was."

"You were just trying to impress me."

"Oh, so you doubt I can wipe out your debt to my store with a keystroke?"

"Of course."

Ambrose took her by the wrist and led her over to his laptop. Calling up her record again he made her watch him type: paid in full with the date. "See, I did it anyway, but just to show you that you were wrong."

"Well, you'd better put it back because I don't intend to have sex with someone within forty-seven minutes of meeting them." She returned to her desert and he followed.

"Look, Paula, I admit it that I shouldn't have rushed things like that." He took the fork out of her hand and began feeding her torte. Then he poured a liberal amount of Amaretto into her coffee.

"Are you trying to get me drunk in the hopes that I'll resume behaving like a slut?"

"You're smart."

"Would you excuse me?" Paula grabbed her purse and suit and marched into the adjoining bathroom. When she emerged, fully dressed, she held the envelope he had given her. "I think I got the envelope intended for your drug dealer."

"Silly. That was allowance for you."

"Allowance?"

"For shopping."

"Is that commonly done in our scene?"

"I'm sure I don't know," he replied shortly, eager to change the subject.

Paula dropped the envelope on an end table.

"Why did you get dressed?"

"I suddenly didn't feel comfortable undressed."

"I simply can't understand the change that's come over you in a few short minutes. You were being so good."

"You mean so bad. So ridiculously easy that you were ready to take me, if I may so express myself, in the most radical way, without so much as a by your leave."

"Every submissive is easy. It's the way you're wired. And besides, what kind of word is that for a liberated woman of the millennium to use? The term easy hasn't been in use since before you were born."

Paula shrugged but allowed him to serve her a fresh coffee and liqueur.

"Got a boyfriend?"

"No."

"No one?"

"I've been seeing a gentleman, but only to play with, not have sex. He's married."

"Does his wife know?"

"Oh, yes. In fact she's the one who urged Hugo to set this date up between us. She's trying to palm me off on you. No pun."

"Well, she had a sensible idea. I'll gladly take you off her husband's hands. In fact, from this day forward, I forbid you to play with that duplicitous rogue."

"Silly. Why should I listen to you?" Paula lit his cigarette.

"Ever live with a man?"

"No and I'm never going to."

"Really?"

"Men are always so delightful. Until they move in. Then all they're good for is making a mess."

"What if you lived in a rich man's house, with servants to clean up the mess?"

"That hasn't been an option so far."

"Maybe it will be some day."

Paula shrugged and sipped her drink.

"That's a good girl," he encouraged her.

"You see, it's all so new to me," she explained in a rush of confidentiality.

"What is, dearest?"

"This business of living out my fantasies. The gentleman I've been playing with has never touched me intimately, no less tried to have sex with me. So you startled me. That's all."

"You've simply been playing what's known as pure B&D,"

127

Ambrose informed her. "But are you sure you want to continue like that?"

"No, but maybe just not go so fast."

"I understand." He took her by the wrist and led her over to the sofa, sat down and pulled her down across his lap. He then pulled up her skirt and down her panties without further preamble.

Paula didn't resist as he refreshed the color in her pearly flesh with his palm.

"You'll never live with a man, will you? I bet I'll have you tied tightly in an apron in a fortnight."

"Is that what you'd like?"

"Why not? I don't think I've ever seen a more perfect bottom."

"Ouch! That's beginning to hurt!"

"You weren't pleased by my caresses, so you'll get this."

"I was pleased."

"But you stopped me."

"Maybe I won't next time."

"You're damn right, you won't."

"You're very bossy, aren't you?"

"You have no idea."

"Won't you go a little lighter? It's becoming sore."

"If you want me to go lighter, spread your thighs."

Paula complied and showed him all her glistening inner pinkness. Delicately but firmly spreading her labia, he inserted one long middle finger into her vagina to the knuckle while she squirmed across his thighs. "There!" Deftly probing for and finding her hitherto undiscovered g-spot, Ambrose gave her a delicious thrill.

"Oh!" she cried in great surprise, never having felt such a quick, easy pleasure before.

Taking his hand away drenched, he began to penetrate her again, only this time plunging two middle fingers into her bottom hole. "I can't wait to dress you up in outfits," he murmured, holding her fast to his lap. "A little sailor suit, for example. With matching navy bloomers to pull down."

"Oh, God," she groaned as he continued to manipulate her deeply. Then abruptly he removed his fingers from her bottom and returned to spanking her hard. This time she didn't complain, but meekly enjoyed every spasm of excitement that pulsed through her.

"Are you ready to go down on your knees to Ambrose?" he asked, spreading her cheeks and emphatically spanking her anus.

"Yes, of course," she cried, without hesitation. Agreeably surprised he made her kneel on the floor between his legs, yanked down his zipper and allowed his massive and handsomely sculpted erection to escape from the tailored confines that had held it in check. Paula's eyes widened but she obediently brought her red lips to the cleanly exposed knob and began to feather it with the tip of her tongue.

"Submissives never know how to give head," he observed, pulling her off, raising her to her feet and leading her to the bed.

"But I was just getting started," she protested.

"Never mind, we'll have a how-to lesson some other time." Pushing her down and rolling her over he shoved a pillow under her tummy and knelt between her thighs. "Don't move," he warned her, finally making use of the condom. Positioning his cock between her slick labia he began to thrust it in. Pulling her up by the hips, he penetrated her one inch at a time. She was very wet and took him to the hilt, in spite of his daunting proportions.

"Please don't let him even dream of putting that huge monster in my bottom," Paula inwardly prayed. The next thing she knew, he was pulling out of her warm, slick pussy and positioning the knob of his engine at her bottom hole. "No!" she cried. "Oh, please, you can't!" She writhed and twisted so that the target seemed to vanish. In frustration he slapped her bottom hard.

"Calm down," he ordered.

"No. I can't take something that big there."

"Nonsense." He spanked her six or eight times in a way that left her gasping. "I'm losing my patience with you."

"Mercy!" she uttered the valuable player's word that David had taught her.

"Damn it, what now?"

"I just can't take you there."

"Stop saying can't." Ambrose held her cheeks apart and spanked her bottom crack until she squirmed. "Tell me when you're ready." Meanwhile he relubricated his penis in her copiously creamy vagina.

"All right!"

"In that case, hold still for me," he ordered, inserting his cock into her anus as slowly as he could. Paula whimpered and sobbed but let him penetrate her anally, miraculously finding that except for the pain of the first sharp, deep thrust, it scarcely hurt at all. "You see? Next time listen to Ambrose." It was quite humiliating how quickly she came.

"This will be the last time I invite you home to tea," Paula sighed as she set the silver service down before David in her apartment several afternoons later.

"It went that well, did it?"

"Mr. Bartlett is unattached, as am I."

"While I'm married and never had any business coming on to you in the first place."

"Of course it will break my heart never to see you again, but Mr. Bartlett is most insistent on that point."

"He would be, the selfish brute."

"I'm sorry." She bowed her pale blonde head.

"No cake?" Accustomed to being showered with petit fours by his hostess, David surveyed the bare tea tray in surprise.

"No cake," Paula tensely replied, eyeing her slim new torso in the mirror opposite. Now that it really mattered she keep the weight off, her craving for sweets had suddenly returned with a violence.

"Sounds like you've got a strict, new master all the way around."

Paula smiled and blushed.

"I'm happy for you darling," he said, fondly kissing her hand. "Still I can't help but resent the efficiency with which my wife and Hugo Sands have torn you from my bosom."

"And I can't blame your bride for being jealous. Frankly I'm amazed at her exemplary handling of the situation."

"That's going to be my lifelong problem with Hope. She handles things."

"I look forward to becoming her friend."

"You girls always stick together."

"Don't be cross."

"I won't be if you do something for me."

"Do what, David?"

"Let me play with you one last time."

"You mean, now?"

"Right now."

"But I gave my word to Ambrose."

"It wasn't fair of him to demand your pledge so quickly."

"He's a forceful gentleman."

"Oh, I see. And what am I?" David got to his feet. "Get up." He pulled her up. "Come over here." He led her over to her most massive armchair and summarily bent her over the arm.

"David! You shouldn't!"

"Don't worry. I'm not going to spank you," he promised soothingly, but pushed her down in the small of her back so that she lay flat across the arm.

"What then?" Paula looked back at him.

"Take you," he replied, flipping up her skirt and pulling down her panties in two swift motions. The next thing she heard was his zipper coming down and a condom coming out of a wrapper.

"David, you shouldn't," she weakly repeated as he spread her legs and labia and nudged his straining erection in between them.

"You're so wet. It will slip in easily." He pushed against her.

"But, I promised Ambrose I wouldn't let you touch me again." She pretended to pull away.

"You're blameless," he assured her, swiftly achieving penetration. "I'm taking complete advantage of you, just as I've always done." He was fully inside her, plunging deeper by the instant, filling her tight glove to the hilt with his engorged cock.

"But we've been so well behaved until this moment," she protested, rocking with his thrusts and squeezing him hard.

"I know. It couldn't last. The longer I abide in Random Point the weaker my resolve becomes."

"Oh!" she cried at a piercing thrust. He reached around and cradled her now nearly flat tummy against the palm of his hand as he drove into her vigorously.

"Dearest Paula," he breathed, pistoning into her velvety sex. "You're such a good girl."

That evening, Ambrose Bartlett sensed something amiss the moment he strode into her domain for the first time. He had come to watch her cook him dinner, bearing lamb chops and basmati rice from the gourmet food section of his store.

"Who was here today?"

"What do you mean?" Paula flushed.

"I detect a faint undertone of cigarette smoke lurking beneath the Caswell Massey room mist. And you don't smoke cigarettes."

"I just started. To help with my diet." To prove it she lifted the lid of an art deco cigarette box and extracted a cigarette.

"The hell you have," he snapped, taking the cigarette away and slapping her sharply on the back of her hand.

"Ow!" she pulled her hand away and nursed it against her cheek.

"I feel as though someone was here today." He followed her into the kitchen.

"Really, Ambrose. This is only our second date. You're acting pretty bossy." Paula began unpacking and setting out the food.

"That man was here, wasn't he?"

"What man?"

Ambrose returned to the sitting room to look for clues. In the kitchen Paula filled pans and turned knobs with an accelerated pulse.

"Paula, get in here this minute!" Ambrose thundered. She ran into the room only to have a Magnum condom wrapper brandished in her face.

"Not my brand of cigarettes. Not my brand of condoms. And even if it was, I've never been here before. Who had you here today and tossed a condom wrapper in the waste basket under the drum table?"

Paula hung her head for the second time that day.

"I see I'm going to have to beat it out of you."

"But, the dinner preparations."

"I thought you weren't seeing anyone."

"I'm not."

"Was it the school teacher?"

"I just had to see him one more time to break it off."

"That's what you call breaking it off, letting him have you?"

"I didn't let him have me. He took me by force."

"I thought you two only played pure B&D?"

"Today it seemed he had to have me."

"Why didn't you repulse him?"

"Because he asked me play one last time and I wanted to."

"And Paula always does exactly what she wants, is that it?"

"Not exactly."

"Never mind. We'll discuss your infidelity later. Go and start the rice now."

Paula stood pouting for a moment. "And mind you put an apron on so you don't ruin that expensive dress." Paula's eyes widened at his tone while his narrowed at her slowness to obey him. "Did you hear me?" he snapped. Paula fled with a pounding heart.

Ambrose strode through the rooms of her home to see how she lived, opening closets and drawers, examining bookshelves and storage bins only to find every compartment in meticulous order. Much impressed, he began to think of Paula as his future wife.

Ambrose walked into the kitchen to find Paula indignant before the linen cupboard. "As if I didn't know enough to put an apron on!" she muttered, her arms folded across the bosom of her crisp khaki shirtwaist with its straight skirt, open collar and three quarter sleeves. Finally she pulled a plain navy apron out and slipped it over her head.

"Let me," he said, coming up behind her to tie her apron strings. She remembered how he'd promised to tie her tightly in an apron within a fortnight and looked at him. For the first time he kissed her.

"I brought you a present," he told her, pulling a flat jeweler's case out of his breast pocket. She opened it with surprise.

"Gold earrings, a necklace and bracelet," she assessed the treasure with delight, stepping in front of a French provincial mirror to change her modest pearls for the heavier, sexier gold ornaments. "Thank you, Ambrose. You have very fine taste."

"Yes."

"But, I thought you were angry with me," she said.

"I am, but I'm still courting you."

"Mercurial, aren't you?" She grinned at him as she assembled spices.

"I was in a bad mood a moment ago," he conceded.

"Have you a jealous nature?"

"Only when I'm madly in love."

She set out gin, vermouth, ice and olives and fondly watched him fill her cocktail shaker.

"I'd be frightened of a jealous lover."

"Why, do you plan to be unfaithful on a regular basis?"

"No, of course not. Never."

"Then you've got nothing to worry about."

"But what if, for example, I looked at or talked to another man?"

"You'll find out."

"How attached are you to that job at Braemar?" Ambrose asked as he watched her set her kitchen to rights after their meal.

"Why do you ask?" She removed the apron at last and took him into the sitting room.

"Look, Paula, I make up my mind quickly. I think we should become engaged. We can have a June wedding and honeymoon in Italy. You'll love the cooking."

"Silly, how can I possibly agree to such a plan after only two dates?"

"Never mind that, I can tell you like the idea."

"Why me?"

"Because you make good coffee."

"You like to shop as much as I do, only you go shopping for people," she observed.

"Honestly, I've never tried to tempt a woman like this before. I was trapped into both my previous marriages. But you, you're like a box of delicious Belgian chocolates that one wants to keep unwrapping."

"But only if I quit my job at Braemar, eh?"

"Why keep a silly job when you'll my wife?"

"You don't want me working around David," she shrewdly

accused her suitor.

"I simply don't enjoy coming home to a work-fatigued woman."

"I never expected a proposal tonight."

"Liar. I should spank you for that."

"But, Ambrose, do you really think that a classic D&S relationship can be maintained over time?"

"If I keep you home it can."

"I like the way that sounds," she uncomfortably admitted.

"Then why look so distressed?" He kissed her lightly on the lips and brushed back her smooth blonde hair.

"Because I feel guilty even considering the possibility."

"You see, that's what's wrong with the millennium. Everything's upside down. Here I suggest the most natural thing in the world, that I take care of you because I love you, and you feel guilty for liking the idea."

"That's because it's been ingrained in me a women must maintain a career, if not two or three all her life."

"Well, of course it's up to you, but since fate tossed you into my lap, I don't think you should fight it." And in so saying he pulled her down on his lap.

"Well, we'll have to see. I don't normally rush into things," she murmured, removing a speck of lint from his silk foulard tie.

"That's okay. I don't mind visiting you here for a while. But don't keep me waiting too long," he warned, firmly patting her bottom.

Chapter Six

Bad Behavior All Around

Determining to separate Marguerite from all temptations, Malcolm Branwell forbid his wife ever to set foot in her bookshop again while Sloan Taylor was its manager. In order to enforce the new rule Malcolm caused her to shut up the house in Random Point and took her back to Boston where he retained a handsome residence.

And this was the reason why Marguerite had still not met Hope Spencer Lawrence, the new resident beauty of Random Point whom Sloan had hired as a clerk at the shop. Hope was being talked of as a jewel and Marguerite was eager to appraise her new employee. But Malcolm cared more about keeping her away from every man in the small Cape Cod village that had ever enjoyed her favors.

Even so, he continued to brood. Kisses, hugs and smiles became dim memories, conversation minimalistic. Sex was hard driving, deliberate and initiated wordlessly, foreplay consisting of Malcolm bending Marguerite over some conveniently curved piece of furniture, pulling her panties off roughly and slapping her hard.

But even sex out of an Ayn Rand novel was not enough to make up for the sudden lack of approbation in Marguerite's life. Having cut her off from everyone, Malcolm also pointedly withheld his own affection. This situation had prevailed for several weeks when the neglected redhead thought of rebelling.

Marguerite had invited Laura Random to Boston for the weekend so her best friend could observe how she suffered. This picture of domestic strife was thoroughly analyzed by Laura, Patricia Fairservis and Laura's sister, Susan Ross as they lunched one afternoon shortly thereafter at The Golden Owl Inn in Woodbridge.

"He barely speaks to her, except sarcastically, uses no endearments, never touches her, except to take her – roughly mind you –" Laura revealed indignantly.

"Yum," Susan cut Laura off.

"– And afterwards he just zips up and walks away," the brunette hotly concluded.

"I can't believe Malcolm Branwell capable of such Gothic behavior," cried Patricia, who now headed the P.R. department of Malcolm's Boston-based bookstore chain.

"I wonder how long he can keep it up," Susan mused. "It sounds kind of sexy."

"You don't know Marguerite if you can say that," Laura corrected her younger sister. "She needs to be adored."

"Then she shouldn't have picked Malcolm," Susan observed.

"Susan, you're not being helpful," Laura chided. "If you could have seen how miserable Marguerite was, trying to please Malcolm in every way, while he ignored her, it would have infuriated you."

"And then he all but he rapes her, does he?" Patricia marveled.

"Yes, well he has to do something to hold her attention," Laura pointed out.

"If he was thoroughly disenchanted with Marguerite he would have just walked out," posited Susan. "His staying on to punish her must mean that he still cares deeply for our friend."

"We should think of some brilliant way to teach him a lesson and at the same time restore him to Marguerite's ample bosom," suggested Patricia.

"There are three of us here, let's concentrate," said Laura. Each of them stirred their tea.

Susan said, "If he's tempted to cheat on her, then they'll be even and he won't be able to feel superior."

"Good idea!" Laura approved.

"So, does anyone here want to volunteer?" Susan asked.

"I'd do it in a heartbeat," said Patricia, "if I didn't working for Malcolm and date Marguerite's ex-boyfriend."

"You're right," agreed Laura, "it would look like you're only interested in Marguerite's men."

"He is the body beautiful though," Patricia fondly mused.

"I'd volunteer if I wasn't so furious at the way he's treating Marguerite," Susan admitted, "but I'm sure my hostility would surface and he'd catch on to our plan."

"Me too. After the way I've seen him behave, I'm more inclined to slap him than let him slap me," Laura replied resolutely.

"What if we were to engage someone else to do it?" Laura suggested.

"Anyone in mind?" Patricia asked.

"Actually, the girl who's working in the bookstore now with Sloan would be perfect."

"Of course," Susan cried, "the glorious Hope Spencer Lawrence. I first met her that time Diana and I went out to Hollywood to play at the B&D club. She's ideal. No man could possibly resist her."

"But would she do it?" Patricia asked, making a mental note to keep Michael Flagg out of the bookstore for the next few years.

"We could try to bribe her. She makes nothing at the bookstore and her husband only earns a teacher's salary. She's already seen Anthony a few times for allowance," Susan informed them.

"But this wouldn't be a straight-forward session. Subterfuge would be involved," Patricia pointed out, "not to mention actual closure."

"You know, that's true," Laura agreed, "and Hope is a newlywed. With a divinely attractive husband who's a little bit strict with her. She might not be willing to seduce a stranger."

"We can ask her anyway. She might enjoy the challenge. And I know she'd appreciate that her sacrifice was in a good cause," Susan declared. "She has a generous spirit. And she's read all of Marguerite's novels. Let me lay the proposition before her."

"Show me the man's photograph," said Hope after Susan unfolded the plan to her over the coffee bar at Marguerite Alexander's bookshop the following day.

"No problem," said Susan, running upstairs to the third floor gallery that housed the most extensive collection of B&D literature in New England. There she found a set of Hugo Sands' New Rod Quarterlies going back several years. She grabbed the relevant issue and ran back down the wooden spiral staircase.

"Here's his picture, with the personal ad that Marguerite first answered." Susan opened to the page with Malcolm's photo, showing him stripped to khaki shorts on the deck of his boat.

"I've ogled that ad before," Hope admitted, "He's delicious."

"Good player too."

"If I accept the assignment it can't be for money. It can only be to help Marguerite," stipulated Hope. "After all, I'm not a courtesan."

"As you know," said Susan, "Marguerite created this wonderful shop and she's passionately attached to it. Malcolm is extremely ungrateful in keeping her away from here, seeing as even he had Marguerite for the very first time upstairs in the third gallery," Susan revealed.

"I suppose that a good deal of sex has been had in the shop," Hope mused as she gazed across the floor to where her handsome young supervisor Sloan Taylor was ringing up sales.

"Yes, the shop has magic," Susan asserted.

"Then this is where I should attempt the seduction," Hope decided.

"Of course, bringing him full circle," Susan eagerly agreed.

"And proving to him that the shop's influence is impossible to withstand if you've a drop of blood in your veins."

"The solution is elegance itself, because if he succumbs to you here, he will then comprehend with crystal clarity how Marguerite managed to succumb to Sloan," Susan thrilled to the plan's symmetry.

"All right. I never come on to men, but I'll make an exception this once, for the sake of my dear boss whom I've never met. But how are we going to get him in here?"

"We'll start by visualizing the event," Susan decided, "That always helps sex occur."

Coincidentally Malcolm's spell of bad temper had just about run its course. One morning, a few days after Susan's discussion with Hope, he looked across the breakfast table and realized that he was forcing himself not to smile at his adorable wife. His dark eyes briefly flickered towards her green ones, realizing with a pang that he'd been positively mean to her for weeks. He cleared his throat and turned a page of The New York Times, attempting to ignore the nagging sensation of guilt that suddenly seemed to choke him.

"I suppose you're just dying to go to Random Point," he said disinterestedly.

"It has been forever," she admitted.

"All right. We'll go for the weekend."

"That would be lovely!"

"Be ready to go by four," he told her, leaving for his office.

No sooner was he out the door than Marguerite was on the phone to Laura.

"Is he still being frigid though?" Laura asked.

"Arctic, as opposed to Antarctic. I seemed to feel a warming trend today."

"Do me a favor. Send Malcolm over to the shop around closing time on Saturday evening. Tell him Sloan won't be there, just the new employee, Hope Lawrence. Ask him to check her out for you to make sure she fits in with the image of the shop."

"But, to what end, Laura? I know that Hope is perfectly well suited to the shop right now."

"Never mind. Four women put their energy into this scheme, so have faith."

Saturday was filled with chores and duties as Marguerite had been away from home for weeks. Towards the middle of that stormy afternoon Malcolm walked into the kitchen, where his wife was painstakingly rolling out a piecrust.

"What are you doing?"

"I'm baking us a shepherd's pie for dinner."

"You seem to be going to a lot of trouble," he commented. "Is there anything I can bring you or errands I can run?"

He seemed so genuinely friendly all at once that she beamed. "I do have a shopping list." She handed him a long one. "And you might buy some flowers and wine. Then, if you can possibly get there before six, I'd love for you to drop those pictures off at the shop." Marguerite indicated an open crate containing six gilt-edged literary portraits.

"Sloan's out of town this weekend, but the new girl will be there," Marguerite added, seeing Malcolm's splendid shoulders stiffen, "and I'd love to hear a report of her."

"Okay," he agreed, grabbing the crate and walking out.

At around ten of six, when Hope had nearly given up on Malcolm visiting, he entered the bookstore with the crate.

"Oh, hello!" she cried, coming forward to meet him. "Aren't you Mr. Branwell?"

Malcolm was astonished to be recognized but even more surprised by the physical perfection of the shop's new clerk. He'd never expected Sloan Taylor, whom he deemed an unprincipled wolf, to hire an unattractive assistant, but Hope Spencer Lawrence was so far at the other end of the spectrum that he was momentarily bereft of speech. Attempting not to stare with too much awe at this flesh and blood personification of a magazine ad, with her two feet of flaxen hair and heavenly waist, he gazed instead into her wide blue eyes and found himself in even greater danger of becoming enthralled. He slid the crate onto a countertop and extended his hand. "You must be Hope Lawrence?"

She warmly shook his hand. "Your photo didn't do you justice, Mr. Branwell."

"Photo?"

"In the magazine."

Malcolm tried to remember the last time his photo had been published. As the youthful CEO of the Branwell's Book Bag chain he had been profiled a number of times, but not in any publication he would have expected Hope to have read.

"Hugo Sands' magazine," she reminded him helpfully.

"Oh!" He colored as he suddenly remembered that Hope was in the scene. Marguerite had mentioned this at a moment when Malcolm had entertained only feelings of resentment towards the shop and the scene. He recalled being more annoyed than intrigued at the time.

"What were you doing reading that?"

"Well, we do carry it here in the shop," she explained, examining the literary portraits in the crate with a racing pulse. She had never seduced a man and hadn't the faintest notion of how to begin. "I've read every issue from cover to cover," she added; so there could be no doubt as to her own orientation. "These portraits are divine. Would you hang them for me?" she asked casually.

"Do you know where you want them?" Malcolm was relieved to get away from the topic of Hugo Sands' magazine and once again shouldered the crate.

"Yes, I think I'll put them in the third gallery!" Hope cried, inspired. Surrounded by erotica and the memories of having first taken Marguerite there, how could he fail to succumb to her own charms in that sacred precinct? "I'll get a hammer and nails and meet you up there!"

Malcolm watched her lock the front door and put out the Closed sign before disappearing into the office, then he climbed the spiral staircase to the third floor with mixed emotions. He remembered the last time he'd been up there. It had been tremendous finally having Marguerite. But he hadn't forgotten that only minutes before he took Marguerite Michael Flagg had been flirting with her on the lower level!

Hope joined him as he laid the pictures on the reading desk. The gallery walls were painted dark green, against which the gold-framed portraits would show richly. Grateful for the time it gave her to think, she carefully directed him as to the placement of the pictures.

"How charming," Hope commented, as the portrait of Charlotte Lennox went up. "Your wife has such exquisite taste!" Malcolm couldn't quite smile in acknowledgement. "How I long to meet her!" Now he positively frowned.

"Which one next?"

"Frances Burney. Right here," Hope indicated a spot. "Why doesn't she ever visit the shop? She and I seem to have so much in common."

"Humph," he grunted, thinking, "If that's true I feel sorry for your husband!"

"I think it's marvelously romantic the way you met through your personal ad."

"Really!" he pronounced the word ironically.

"I think it's the height of good breeding to meet through a correspondence. My husband was compelled to beat a much cruder path to my door," Hope revealed.

"Oh?"

"He found me working in a B&D club in Hollywood."

"So, was that your last position before coming here?" Malcolm was scandalized.

"No. Just prior to coming back East I'd quit The Keep and was doing movies. Then David got offered the teaching post at Braemar and invited me to accompany him here as his wife. Wasn't that romantic?"

"Which one's next?" Malcolm asked, hammer and nail fixture in hand.

"Elizabeth Inchbald. Place her just to the right of Frances Burney, please," Hope directed, stepping back to study the effect. "I understand you're practically a newlywed yourself?"

"Practically," he replied in a tone devoid of warmth.

"Better move that one over to the left another inch."

"Are you sure?"

"Uh-huh," murmured Hope, studying the dramatic vee formation of his shoulders and waist when he turned to hammer the nail. While she was growing fonder of his physique by the moment, she felt increasingly self-conscious about initiating the planned mischief. Damn him for his polite indifference to her brilliant pheromones.

"You must have received dozens of answers to your ad," she returned to the subject of Malcolm with renewed zest. She had thought of her assignment as simply doing a good deed for a goddess but now it had become an artistic challenge. Unlike her alley cat of a husband, this modest and sincere married male would never be the first to make a move.

"I got a few."

"I'll bet your heart nearly stopped when Marguerite's was one of them," Hope guessed ingenuously.

"Now look," he suddenly snapped, causing her heart to contract, "I'm sure you're a very nice person and mean no harm, but you've been asking some very impertinent questions and I think you'd better stop."

"I'm sorry!"

"Who's next?" he gestured at the art.

"Oh, Maria Edgeworth. Line her up about three inches below Charlotte Lennox, please." Hope paced as he hammered the nail. The pictures were going up fast and she was no nearer to winning him over. Just the opposite! He seemed irritated with her. "Please forgive me if I offended you," she murmured.

"You didn't offend me."

"If I seemed too familiar it's only because I know that you're in the scene. Just that one fact seems to promote intimacy. I guess you don't agree?"

"I never thought about it."

"That's your problem," she blurted out.

"I beg your pardon?"

"Never mind."

"I want to know what you meant by that remark," he persisted.

"I can't elaborate without being even more impertinent."

Malcolm straightened Maria Edgeworth's portrait with a critical eye. "My wife forced me to read a book by her once," he admitted mildly. "Not bad."

"I like your wife!" cried Hope enthusiastically. "Oh, how I wish you'd let her be my friend!"

Malcolm felt himself becoming angry. Unaware of how rapidly information could be disseminated within a clique, he was astonished that this shop girl, a total stranger to him until minutes ago, should know so much about his relationship with Marguerite. It was also humiliating to be reproached for what even he was beginning to consider his unfair repression of his wife by this infuriating brat.

"And oh, how I wish I had the authority to fire you for being so fresh!" he declared.

Hope went pale and red by degrees. Suddenly she also felt angry. She was about to retort but tears filled her eyes and she turned her back on him to compose herself. When he noticed the shoulders of her dove grey cardigan tremble he felt an unpleasant spasm of guilt.

"Sensitive, aren't you?" he brusquely observed.

"I'll be happy to resign," she whimpered, wounded nearly beyond words.

"Oh, don't be silly."

"You don't know me and I was forward with you," Hope excoriated herself.

He suddenly felt what a cad he was being. "Look, I didn't mean what I said. I'm sure the shop is lucky to have you. Will you forgive me for upsetting you? Please?"

Hope turned to him and smiled. "Yes, thank you." Then she ingeniously added, "Will you show me that you forgive me too by giving me a hug?" Without allowing him to decide, she threw her arms around his slim waist and pressed her fair head to his chest, breathing a sigh of contentment. Malcolm felt it was very wrong, but couldn't help locking his own arms around the bewitching beauty, who did not seem inclined to release him for some moments. When she pulled back it was to look up into his eyes with frank admiration. "I love when I can feel a man's rib cage."

"That's nice but I think you'd better stop now," he advised, pulling her hands away. However, he could not quite bring himself to relinquish them at once. "You know, I'm beginning to think that you're a very naughty girl." He let her go and went back to hanging the remaining two portraits. "I assume Jane Austen is next?"

"Yes, please."

"I wonder what your husband would say if he knew that you went around fondling other men's rib cages."

Hope laughed, "He wouldn't say anything."

"Right!"

"That looks good. Now put Anne Bronte up just to her right."

"Suppose the situation were reversed and I squeezed your waist? Would you consider that acceptable behavior?"

"Highly!" she readily assented, bringing up his color again. "But why stop there?"

"Mrs. Lawrence, I'm beginning to get the impression that you're flirting with me," Malcolm pronounced disapprovingly.

"Is that so terrible?"

"Considering we're both married, yes."

"Aren't you ever spontaneous?"

"If I did what I really feel like doing right now you wouldn't like it," he asserted bluntly, putting the last picture up.

"You mean fire me?"

"No, turn you over my knee!"

"Oh!" Hope blushed, having almost forgotten that option in her unadulterated lust for his athletic body.

"However, I don't chastise other men's wives," he told her, standing back from the portrait to judge his job.

"You know, you're impossibly stuffy! It's really hard for me to believe that you're even in the scene, no less husband to the divine Marguerite Alexander. I've heard about straight-laced New Englanders but always thought they were a Hollywood cliché. Don't you realize the millennium is here?"

Malcolm regarded her for a long moment. "God, I'd enjoy spanking you for your insolence!"

"But you just don't dare, do you?" she mocked him, weary of attempting to seduce him. "Because then you would have touched a girl and you couldn't lord it over Marguerite that you were so pure and she so abandoned!"

Malcolm thought of slapping her face but good manners held him in check.

"I just realized something. You're stuck on my wife!"

"Really, Mr. Branwell, what a thing to say," she weakly protested, cursing herself for blurting the recrimination out.

"You just used the word abandoned with regard to Marguerite. Thank you for opening my eyes. Compared to you, she's a Catholic saint. At least she has to know a man three or four weeks before committing adultery."

She calmly swept the hammer and nails into a drawer in the reading table, then sat on the table to look at the job he had done. "I can't believe how fast you put those up," she remarked, feeling her face begin to burn with embarrassment at the way she had failed in her task. She had never in her life had so little effect on a healthy male.

"As I said, you do need a good spanking, but I'm going to let your husband give it to you," Malcolm announced with resolve.

"My husband? What do you mean?" Hope cried, her heart contracting painfully.

"Do you know what this shop is, Hope? It's a breeding ground for marital infidelity. But you and I are going to break the cycle!"

"Yes, of course, but what did you mean when you mentioned my husband?"

"At least I'm going to break the cycle," he amended, remembering that that unprincipled seducer of married women, Sloan Taylor still ran the shop and was Hope's superior. "You've probably already been down on your knees to your boss," he accused with cruel derision.

"Nothing of the sort," she replied unsteadily, "but what did you mean about my husband? You did mention him just now."

"I intend to send him a letter informing him of his wife's outlandish behavior."

"You're joking."

Hope followed Malcolm downstairs, turning out lights behind them as they went, her knees like water. "You really don't intend to do that, Mr. Branwell, do you?"

"You're afraid of your husband, I see. Good! I hope he beats the daylights out of you."

"Mr. Branwell, you can't mean that!" she nearly sobbed. "I mean, think of his feelings. Be a sport."

This exhortation weakened his resolve, but he was enjoying her humility and pleading far too much to let her know she'd gained an edge.

"Good night, Mrs. Lawrence," Malcolm said, striding out the front door, whereupon Hope immediately burst into tears. Not only had she failed in her mission, but now she was going to have a note written home to David! It simply didn't bear thinking of.

"Well, you may or may not be happy to know that you've got a 100% bona fide tart working for you at the bookstore," Malcolm matter of factly announced to Marguerite as he unpacked groceries in the kitchen of her house on the tip of Random Point several minutes later. Marguerite turned to him as she gingerly removed the shepherd's pie from the oven, steam rising from the punctures in the crust.

"What do you mean?"

"I mean that Hope Spencer Lawrence is an unrepentant thrill-seeker with no more respect for her own marriage vows than anyone else's, least of all yours."

"I don't understand."

"I hadn't been in the shop ten minutes before she began coming on to me."

"Coming on to you?"

"As I was putting up the pictures she began to needle me."

"Needle you about what?"

"Our relationship!" he coldly returned. "She's pretty well informed about it."

Marguerite bit her lip but changed the subject. "Is she as attractive as I've heard?"

"Stunning. But of course she'd have to be to get away with half her nonsense."

"Tell me more about what happened."

"Well, after she got a good rise out of me and I responded by telling her off, she proceeded to squeeze out a couple of tears, which of course turned me to butter. During the consolation stage she heavily turned on the charm, giving me to understand that spontaneity was her idol. There wasn't a doubt in my mind that I could have had her then and there. I tell you, it made me so mad, I almost spanked her."

"Almost? That doesn't sound like you."

"Marguerite! You're just as bad as she is. In fact, you really are two of a kind!" he declared, pacing with his hands in the pockets of his khakis. "Oh, and by the way, she worships you. Worships you and yet feels no compunction about putting the make on your husband! Can you even begin to comprehend such a twisted mentality?"

"Worships me?" Marguerite smiled.

"You don't even care that she came on to me, do you?"

"If she couldn't help herself."

"How could she not help herself? I'm a married man. She's a married woman. We'd met two minutes before in a semi-public place. How could she not help herself?"

"If she found you so attractive as to be irresistible."

"Are you saying that you wouldn't be upset, disturbed or in the least bit jealous if I were to make love to another women? And a beauty at that?"

"I'm saying nothing of the kind. I'm sure I would be jealous if I thought you did make love to her, especially if she's a glorious as everyone says she is. But not if you just spanked the naughty flirt."

"Humph!"

"You really should have spanked her. I'm sure that's what she wanted."

"And how do you think her husband would feel if he found out about it?"

"Perhaps he's the liberal type."

"We'll see how liberal he is after he's been apprised of the situation."

"Malcolm, you aren't going to tell him!"

"Maybe after she's had a sharp lesson from her husband she'll think twice before accosting strangers as she did me."

"Malcolm you couldn't possibly be so cruel as to report her misbehavior to her husband. He might be terribly hurt."

"Better now than later, after she's trampled on every marriage vow she ever made."

"But, Malcolm, this isn't funny. We have no idea of what Mr. Lawrence may be like. He could really be the violent type. You don't want to be responsible for Hope getting a black eye, do you?"

"Oh, Marguerite, don't be ridiculous. Hope's a spoiled rotten little slut."

"Still, why not think it over a couple of days before you do something rash?" Marguerite urged, cutting him a slice of pie.

"I can't understand why you have the slightest degree of sympathy for that brat. Mm, this is good. It tastes very rich though," he commented with disapproval.

"You can indulge yourself slightly for once," she fondly observed, pouring his tea. "Surely you used up your daily ration of puritanical self-denial in refusing to enjoy Hope Spencer's charms?"

"There must be a thousand calories in one slice of this," he speculated.

The small seed of lust that Hope had planted in Malcolm's brain germinated overnight to the point that he awoke the following morning with a raging erection, having dreamt of her corn silk blonde hair. It was another rainy day. Marguerite was already downstairs brewing coffee as he sat up with a start and tried in vain to recapture the elusive wisps of dream that were quickly floating out of his mind.

He showered and dressed in confusion, wanting nothing more than to stroll directly over to the bookshop and immediately claim all that had been so casually offered to him the previous day.

"I think I'll go out for some bagels," he told Marguerite on his way out the door.

"Okay, dear," she called from the kitchen.

Malcolm walked through the village under a big, black umbrella, hoping that Sloan would still be out of town and Hope manning the store. He found her alone in the shop, dressed in a white shirt and jeans under her cranberry apron, polishing the antique espresso maker while humming along to the 1924 cast album of Funny Face playing on a Victoria in the corner.

"Mr. Branwell!" she cried with a blush as he walked in the door.

"Anyone here?" he asked, looking around.

"No."

"In that case we're closed for lunch," he told her, turning the sign in the front window around and locking the door. Then he strode over to the cappuccino bar and pulled her out from behind it by the wrist. "We have unfinished business," he told her, dragging her to the back of the shop, behind the back counter and into the office where he deposited her on the leather sofa before locking the door.

"Mr. Branwell, what in the world are you about?" she cried, jumping up. But he pushed her down again and sat down too. "I thought over everything you said and decided that it would be madness to repress my urge to spank you for a moment longer." And in so saying he took her by the arm and pulled her straight across his lap. The dark red apron strings framed her bottom in the jeans as cutely as could be, but the roundness of her cheeks had to be squeezed to be fully appreciated.

"Mr. Branwell, you're so different today!" she exclaimed, inwardly rejoicing at having worn her newest, darkest blue jeans, against which the sweep of her long fair hair looked particularly handsome as she lay across his powerful thighs.

He began to spank her with short, fast, warm-up smacks that were hard enough to elicit whimpers from Hope.

"Well I thought it over and realized that you deserve many spankings, not just ones from your husband. So in a sense I'm helping."

Now the spanks came slower and harder. The jeans kept in the heat, but he could feel it coming through them. An experienced submissive, Hope rapidly fell under the hypnotic spell of the falling smacks and ceased to whimper.

"Lift up," he ordered and when she did, he unbuttoned and unzipped her jeans and deftly slipped his hand into her panties to capture her sex in his palm. Then pressing his hand against her Venus mound and slit, he continued with the spanking though her jeans.

"My God, what are you doing?"

"I just want to feel you get wet."

"Oh! How dare you!" She tried to wriggle away from his hand but he held her fast. Five or six more smacks fell on her snugly denimed backside.

"Hold still, you. It's a bit late to start playing the prude."

Hope didn't know whether to say "Ow!" or "Oooooh!" as he lightly entwined his finger tips in her dewy pubic curls while simultaneously smacking her bottom ever more resoundingly. Harder and faster he spanked her while holding her sex in the palm of his hand. Finally he allowed one slender finger to slip up into her vaginal canal, which instantly clung like a wet, velvet sheath. At the same time he yanked her jeans down, along with her thin white cotton panties, to bare her pink-on-cream silken cheeks.

Ceasing to masturbate her, he held her fast around the waist and continued the spanking resolutely, covering her small, round bottom with score upon score of sharp smacks.

Hope passively submitted, transported by his firm but sensual techniques. She enjoyed the way he reached under her and deliberately divided her labia before pressing her back down against his olive twill trousers.

Then he took her one step further, by deliberately spreading her pinkened cheeks and spanking in between them.

Hope couldn't help but gasp when he spanked her anus.

"I couldn't stop thinking of you the entire night," he reported at length.

She shifted and the tiny target disappeared. She squirmed and twisted, broke his hold and seated herself upright on his lap.

"You thought of me?" she cried, wrapping her arms around his neck and nuzzling his throat with her cheek. "Thank you for telling me that! I thought you despised me when you walked out of here yesterday."

"I just wanted to wring your neck."

"You wanted to tell my husband how I had outraged your decency," she smiled, jumping off his lap to pull up her jeans.

"Oh, I never really meant to do that."

"Really? I was so certain that you would that I went home and made a full confession to David."

"I'm sure you did not such thing!"

"You shouldn't be so sure of everything. I would have told him anyway. It might have been a day; it might have been a week. But I'd have blurted it out."

"And what happened?"

"I don't think I'll tell you."

"No, really, how did he take it? I'm curious about how other men react to such behavior."

Hope straightened her apron and hair in the art deco mirror that looked so well in Sloan's office. "Well, unlike you, David has a sense of humor. Though he said it served me right for thinking I was irresistible to men."

"Is that all he said or did?"

"Must I really reveal how I was punished by my husband?" She pouted so deliciously that he could no longer resist the impulse to take her in his arms and kiss her full, red mouth.

Hope gasped when Malcolm finally let her go.

"You're a sweet girl. I'm sorry I didn't realize that yesterday. I hope you didn't get in too much trouble."

"Oh, David doesn't take things too seriously," Hope admitted thankfully.

"Good," said Malcolm, pulling her back into his arms to kiss her again.

"What's going on?" she asked, in a daze from his bruising kisses. "You changed."

"Just consider yourself lucky you're not wearing a skirt," he warned her, fondling her waist as well as her firm, little, apple-round bosom through the apron and shirt. "I could bend you over and be in you in a second." He pulled her hard against him again, breathed in the faint perfume of her hair and squeezed her bottom through the jeans with both hands while fastening his lips to her throat. She luxuriated in his deep kisses for several minutes, feeling like a woman on the cover of a bodice-ripper.

"I could kneel and give you head," she suggested, at length, "And you could correct me with your belt."

Malcolm sat on the leather sofa and she knelt between his legs to watch him unbuckle his belt and pull it free. Doubling it he motioned for her to unzip his trousers. Hope did this without hesitation for her animal spirits were running high that day and she'd dreamt of Malcolm all night. She found his erection daunting as it sprang into her hand.

"What a beautiful cock," she murmured. "Now I really wish I'd worn a skirt too." For she hated the thought of being bent over and taken with her jeans inelegantly around her ankles, nor could she see herself stripping in Sloan's office in the middle of a work day for a romp on the leather sofa with the owner's husband.

"That's why you're being punished." He began to strap her lightly, not too certain it was safe to do otherwise with his organ between her teeth.

"Mm, a little harder would teach me a better lesson," she prettily begged, for the strap felt divine through her jeans and made the act of servicing him while fully dressed exquisitely submissive.

Five minutes of this and he was ready to relinquish all claim the moral high ground in his marriage and discharge passionately. Hope sensed the subtle indications of the coming deluge and pulled away just in time to miss being choked or drenched by Malcolm's liquid tribute as it harmlessly fell on the soil of a potted palm several feet away.

"You little darling," he told her, kissing her head before pulling her to her feet.

"You big bruiser," she teased fondly.

He took her in his arms and held her close, all his resentment and confusion about Random Point evaporating into the cedar scented atmosphere of Sloan's office.

Hope was pleased, feeling she'd done a good thing for both her boss and the scene. But late that afternoon, her husband strode into the shop with a look on his face that told her she'd outsmarted herself.

Without much preamble, David took Hope by the ear and dragged her into the back of the store, where he threw her into the first open doorway her came to, which was Sloan Taylor's office, where she'd given Malcolm Branwell such a thrill earlier that day.

Accusations issued from her husband's handsome mouth as concisely as might be expected. It seemed he'd made one of his rare visits to the gym in search of a game of squash. There he encountered Malcolm Branwell, who introduced himself to David and accepted the challenge. David presently discovered that Malcolm was the husband of the owner of the bookshop where Hope worked, Marguerite Alexander Branwell. David then revealed he was the husband of Marguerite's employee, Hope Lawrence. Hearing this, Malcolm Branwell was at first flustered, then confiding.

Naturally, David was not surprised to be complimented on his bride, to hear her looks compared to those of the young Grace Kelly and her manners described as charming. What disturbed him was Malcolm's subsequent remarks about how much he admired David for being so evolved about Hope's unabashed availability. This statement leaving David speechless, Malcolm added quickly that Hope had explained about how she shared everything with her husband, or he never would have said a word. Indeed, he would have felt extraordinarily uncomfortable even confronting David.

Playing along, David had agreed that it was wonderful how Hope told him everything, while Malcolm lamented the fact that his wife told him nothing. David said perhaps there was nothing to tell, which made Malcolm laugh. Then Malcolm beat David at squash and they parted on a friendly note, after which David had come directly to the bookstore.

David sat on the edge of Sloan's desk and crooked his finger at his wife, who blushed and hung back. But the office was small enough for him to reach out for her wrist and yank her straight across his knee.

"Hope, what does Malcolm Branwell think you told me?"

"You want to converse with me like this?"

Smack! Smack! Smack! "Answer the question, Hope."

"No. Let me go! I will not be interrogated like this! And David, the store is still open for business. What if a customer came in?"

"If a customer comes in, we'll hear the bell and I'll let you go."

"How can we hear the tiny tinkle of the bell with you whacking away at me with all your might?'

"What did Malcolm mean when he used the term 'unabashed availability' with regard to my dear wife?"

"I suppose it was just something he inferred from my conversation," Hope suggested, trying for a more comfortable position as she dangled in mid-air. David resumed spanking her in a most unpleasant style.

"Hope, did you come on to Malcolm?"

She was momentarily reprieved by the tinkle of the bell. "I may have flirted a little," she blushingly revealed before running out to attend to the customer.

The shop was closing in fifteen minutes. Hope busied herself with all the usual chores while David paced the aisles impatiently. When six o'clock struck he himself ushered the lone browser out, put up the closed sign and locked the door.

Hope was not so easily corralled this time and he had to chase her around the first floor and up the stairs before finally catching her on the third gallery landing. Hope attempted to marshal her thoughts as David seized her by the forearm and thrust her down across the reading table, pinning her by the waist and using his other hand to renew the warmth in her jeans.

"You're not supposed to be flirting," he advised her, bringing his palm down hard across either cheek repeatedly. "You're a married woman now. Remember?"

"Of course, David. Naturally. I think about it all the time."

"Then why approach your boss's husband?" David stopped spanking her to let her reply.

"It's a long and complicated story," Hope explained, reaching back to rub her bottom.

"I've got time."

"But we have to get home. I have to cook dinner and –"

"I want to hear the long and complicated story," David told her, reaching under her to unbuckle her belt and lower her zipper. Like the proper submissive she was, Hope sighed and stayed in position as he pulled down her blue jeans and panties to mid-thigh. He found her stunning bottom already creamy pink from his hand. Pressing her against the table hard he began to loudly smack her and stain her cheeks magenta with his punishing palm.

Hope sighed again. When he pressed her down against the table a thrill rippled through her that nearly triggered an actual climax, but the pain of the slaps that followed all but blocked the sexual charge. Hope cried out but he ignored her, renewing his grip on her waist.

Becoming more accustomed to the rhythm of his arm she succumbed to its seductive power and began to experience spasms of pleasure in spite of the pain. Somehow being held down for a spanking, in just the right way, sent her into transports. She communicated the effect he was having upon her with whimpers and pants.

No man ever being proof against Hope in a state of excitement, least of all her husband, David relented and let her up, drawing her into his arms. Kissing and fingering her he determined she was ready and wet.

Bending her over the desk, David entered Hope from behind. The indignity of being taken with her jeans around her ankles did not please her but the throbbing in her clitoris cried out for appeasement.

"I can't believe you flirt with other men!" He drove into her hard and spanked her for good measure. Hope could only sob with sexual emotion and grip the edge of the desk as he took her with abandon.

"It was for a very good cause," she explained, some minutes later, as they set their clothes to rights, counting herself lucky to get off so easily, having been so very wayward that day.

Chapter Seven

Michael Finds Hope

Michael Flagg and Hope Spencer Lawrence had been eyeing each other for several weeks like characters out of a James M. Cain novel.

It began the first time he came in for breakfast and immediately found that watching the girl in the cranberry apron manipulate an Italian espresso machine was something in the nature of an aesthetic experience. The shapely blue-jeaned bottom, the marvelous corn silk hair to even more heavenly waist and the perfume emanating from every well groomed pore – compelled Michael fall in love with the new book shop clerk even before she turned to reveal her remarkably beautiful face.

Hope would reflect upon it later as a Romance channel moment. Michael looked at her and was dazzled, while she gazed up at him as at a god.

Slowly sinking onto the counter stool, Michael couldn't turn his gaze from the new Lorelei of Random Point as she delivered the latte she'd just prepared to a customer by the fireplace.

"You work here?" he demanded when she slipped back behind the cherry wood counter.

"Certainly I do," she extended her hand. "I'm Hope."

"Michael."

He noticed her wedding band with a twinge of unease. However, he was back the next day. And every one thereafter. Soon she began anticipating nine-fifteen a.m. with excitement.

"Of course I'm still painfully in love with my husband," Hope talked to herself in the mirror. "But that doesn't mean I'm impervious to the charms of a Celtic warrior king in perfect tweeds."

Even loving David as she did, seeing Michael Flagg was wanting him and feeling as tenderly toward him as she did, she couldn't resist smiling at him one extra time per visit, or cutting him much larger slices of German apple pie than she ought to have done.

One dark, rainy October day, she arrived at the shop in a wool skirt and cashmere sweater set, set off by pearls and leather pumps. No one had ever seen Hope with her hair up before and the change was profound. Sloan, Hope's boss, a sophisticated young man with a better understanding of the female sex than most, could see what was going on.

After Michael left Sloan scolded her, "You'd better be careful."

"I'll cut a thinner slice next time."

"I mean of Michael Flagg."

"Why?"

"You ought to ask around before getting involved."

"Ask who?"

"Start with your friends and neighbors."

"Why?"

"Hope, you have a tolerant husband but don't you think you're going too far?"

"Why? Nobody stopped David when he had that affair with Miss Rohan."

"Yes they did, you stopped him. You set her up with Mr. Moneybags over in Woodbridge."

"I saw a need to act swiftly. As it turns out, she's much better off. I hear they're getting married."

"Just be careful you don't fall in love," Sloan firmly lectured.

"I'm already in love. With David."

"I think I must inform you that Michael was the one that got away from our Marguerite."

"No!" Hope felt her heart lurch. This dreadful pronouncement changed everything. "But she's married to Mr. Branwell now."

"Sure, but she had a secret affair with Michael as recently as a few months ago."

"Doesn't sound like much of a secret."

"Well, I was her confidante at the time. Believe me, it would pain

Marguerite greatly if you were to enter into any sort of liaison with Michael Flagg without her approval."

"Thank you for telling me that."

"Besides, think of David. Shame on you, Hope. You're a very bad girl."

"Why?"

"How does David defend your honor against a rival like Michael Flagg?"

"You don't know David. 'What honor?' he'd snap with that condescending glare in his eye that I find so endearing."

Hope invited Susan Ross and her older sister Laura to the cottage for tea one rainy afternoon just a few days before Halloween for the purpose of grilling them about Michael Flagg.

"He's a god," reported Susan.

"That's what I thought!" Hope breathed.

Laura said, "All the girls love Michael."

"Even Marguerite?"

"Especially Marguerite!" said Laura and Susan in unison.

"And is the goddess jealous of the god?" Hope asked.

"Have you ever heard of a goddess who wasn't?" asked Susan. "Why? Are you thinking of making yourself available to Michael?"

"He's been coming in for breakfast every single day. Sometimes staying an hour."

"He must be watching your snugly denimed bottom swishing around behind the counter." Susan decided.

"I'm sure that's part of it," Hope agreed.

"Want to hear a stunning fact about Michael?" Susan asked, then continued, "He used to be married to a girl in the scene named Damaris, who when she ran away and left him, wound up at The Keep in Hollywood, in which he tracked her down and thrashed her, in Bishop." Susan named one of the dungeons in the club where Hope had worked for a year and where Susan had played at working once for a couple of days, which was when she and Hope had first met.

"It certainly is a small B&D world," Hope marveled.

"But in spite of the romantic rescue, the marriage didn't last," said

Laura, "Damaris is now living with my ex-husband. And Michael is free."

"But you're not," Susan reminded Hope.

"I don't suppose Michael ever pays for sessions?" Hope threw out idly. "David lets me do sessions."

"Yes, make Michael pay for sessions!" Susan thought this hilarious.

"Don't laugh! I've had many a beautiful male pay for the privilege of dominating me," Hope replied with hauteur.

"I think it's a fine idea," Laura approved.

"So, have you two ever played with him?" Hope shyly threw out.

"I've played with him twice," Laura confessed.

"I spent a night with him once," said Susan with unabashed pride.

"From your expressions I can tell that you both just hated it," Hope commented.

"We've been in love with Michael for years."

"So why did his wife run away?"

"She found out he had cheated on her with Marguerite," Laura supplied. "Apparently she did not consider this a supportable insult. To Damaris it was reason enough to divorce."

"So why didn't Marguerite grab him as soon as he was free?" Hope wondered.

Marguerite answered Hope's question herself the first time they were alone together in the shop.

"I hoped he would propose. But he never did," she sighed. "Then all of a sudden, he seemed to have a new girl friend. So finally I gave up on him."

"Oh? He has a girlfriend?" Hope's heart contracted painfully.

"She's out of town for the winter."

Hope's shoulders untensed and she gently asked, "So you gave up on Michael and married Mr. Branwell?"

"That is so," replied Marguerite.

Hope threw another log on the fire. It was another wet, blustery day and she couldn't stand close enough to the hearth. "Tell me more about Michael?"

"Where do you know him from?"

"He's been coming in for breakfast every morning."

"Really? Just you and him across the counter?" Marguerite asked casually.

"He always has two double cappuccinos and a sesame cream cheese bagel with tomatoes."

"How long has this been going on?"

"Eleven consecutive days."

Marguerite blushed and her heart beat fast. "Sounds like the boy's in love."

"One can't help but be tempted," Hope observed.

"A darling man once said that the only way to get rid of a temptation was to yield to it," Marguerite judiciously allowed.

Now Hope had everyone's permission except her husband's to pursue the strappingly handsome, former-detective whose blue eyes had pierced her soul. The next morning when he slid onto his customary stool Michael instantly sensed a change. Hope was in a straight skirt, open-collared blouse with pushed up sleeves, high heels, her long blonde mane in a pony tail, with her lips and nails dark red. Her delicious waist encircled by a broad leather belt, could not have looked daintier. And there was nothing but mischief in her eyes.

Michael smiled as she set his cappuccino down and started preparing his order. She returned the smile seductively, the bad girl off a pulp fiction cover.

"How I wish you weren't married," he grumbled, as she placed a silver knife and spoon on his white cloth napkin.

"Why? What would you do?"

"Court you."

"Some people speak highly of your courtship techniques."

"Really? You've been talking to the locals about yours truly?"

"Just a few mutual friends who all gave you the highest endorsements." Hope decorated Michael's plate with fresh cucumber slices and butter lettuce.

"Endorsements?"

"As a player," Hope informed him.

"A player?" Michael wasn't sure he'd heard her correctly.

"A first rate dominant," Hope elucidated, though in a soft, confidential tone.

"You're in the scene? This is too good to be true."

"I thought you were a detective. You've been flirting with me for eleven days and you never bothered to ask around about me?"

"You're right, that's not like me," Michael agreed.

"My husband still allows me to do sessions," Hope said helpfully.

"Sessions? You?"

"Sure. David first met me at The Keep in Hollywood."

"You're kidding. I've been there."

"Yeah, I heard you gave your wife a good licking in Bishop. I find that painfully exciting."

Michael leaned his chin on his hand and simply gazed at her. "You have a lovely way with words," he complimented her before addressing the colorful platter she'd placed before him with enthusiasm. "A great weight has been lifted from my conscience, Hope dear," Michael confided, cutting his sandwich into quarters.

"Really?"

"The husband thing was bothering me. That's the only reason I haven't approached you. But what you've told me changes everything."

"Imagine how thrilled I was to be told that spanking is your fetish, I couldn't stop thinking about going submissive to you," Hope confided sincerely.

"I'd love to engage you for a session."

"Are you serious?"

"If it was fun we could make it a regular thing," Michael suggested.

"You're making this too easy."

"Come to my house on your day off."

"That's tomorrow."

"Come."

"Write down your address." Hope passed him a card and a pen.

"Will you come?"

"Write down your phone number."

"Come at three."

"Good."

"Thunderstorms thrill me," said Hope, curled up in the window seat of Michael Flagg's sitting room the following day while thick sheets of rain washed the house. "And you look like you were drawn by Tom of Finland, may he rest in peace," Hope added of her host's gracefully athletic and overwhelmingly virile appearance in the black levis and a black knit shirt which displayed his arms and torso in all their marbled glory.

While Hope in a herringbone skirt, nipped at the waist by a chunky black belt, over a stiff, white crinoline, and a white open collared blouse with the sleeves rolled to the elbows was Sweet Gwendolyn to a seam. Michael could scarcely take his eyes off his lithe guest in her sheer black hose and 4" pumps.

"I love what that belt does to your waist," he murmured endearingly.

"I've thought of feeling your hands around it," Hope admitted.

"I've thought of putting them there," he said, lifting her out of the window seat and transporting her to the love seat opposite the fireside. He sat down with Hope in his lap and kissed her as he'd wanted to since the moment they'd met.

The kiss alone lasting ten minutes, it seemed to Hope that Venus would be their ruling star. "Let's break with convention," she erred by putting her thought into words.

"What do you mean?" Michael's hand under her frothy petticoat was already venturing to fondle the silken inner portions of her bare thighs above her stocking tops. Subsequently Hope could only whimper as his deft fingertips caressed her through her panties.

"Hope? You started to say something."

Instead of replying she let him kiss her throat and behind her perfumed ears, which made her feel ticklish and wriggle on his lap. Presently his fingertips slipped into her panties and his tongue into her mouth.

"It's just that I'm so ready now," she murmured.

"Ready?"

"I'm an artist and a free spirit. Therefore I see no reason for you not to take me right now!"

"Take you? During a session? I thought well bred girls didn't permit that."

"Michael, you know the session thing is only an excuse that I can give to my husband as to why I'm here with you today. If there was any other way for me to legitimately see you -- I mean without offending David, I'd suggest it."

"Maybe we can do a double date thing one night. I'll bring over a submissive girl and we can switch partners."

"Great. Meanwhile, let me get a condom." Hope jumped off his lap, went to her purse and retrieved a Rough Rider.

"You're going to give yourself to me on our first date?" Michael took her back on his lap and locked his arms around her.

"When David finds out what you look like he might not let me have a second. Besides, I always live each day as though it were my last. It's a Hollywood thing."

"But I liked the idea of having sessions with you," he put her off his lap and made her stand in front of him. "It insures that you'll obey all orders meekly and even submit to humiliations, virtually without question. Just because it pleases me."

"Oh? You'd rather play pure B&D than possess me body and soul?" Hope drew back indignantly.

"If you're not really submissive, maybe I don't want to possess you body and soul."

"Oh?"

"If you've just come for regular sex..."

"Yes?"

"That would be a lot less interesting."

Hope blushed in mortification, remembering that dominant men sometimes resented submissive women making suggestions.

"I'm sorry," she replied, without meeting his eyes. "I was drawn to you sexually. So I wanted to feel you inside me."

"Hope, go stand in the corner," he ordered with a parting smack. "And don't think that I won't punish you for making such inappropriate suggestions."

"I figured," she murmured, turning her face to the wall, but peeking back over one shoulder.

"I have no desire to alienate a wife from her husband," Michael stated staunchly.

"Then why did you French kiss me and knead my bosom in that charming way just now?"

"I'll ask the questions, young lady."

"You slipped your fingers into my panties," she added.

"So? I suppose a man can take a few liberties with a submissive who behaves the way you do."

Hope's face grew warm as she stared at the wall, wishing she could go ten or so minutes back in time and behave more demurely.

Calling her back to him he proceeded to behave exactly as he ought to. He took her over his knee and spanked her in a style that stamped him for a true enthusiast.

Analyzing his approach and much too excited to even feel the first few dozen swats, Hope saw that a mirror directly opposite the big, armless chair where he chose to execute her punishment, reflected her face, Michael's profile and his arm rising and descending unremittingly. The motion picture of herself being spanked by Michael charmed her beyond bearing and Hope fluttered with excitement every time she saw him strike, which was often.

"I thought you'd enjoy looking at yourself," he remarked. Hope pouted. Did everyone really think she was as vain as David insisted?

Hope remembered her last discussion with David on the subject of her vanity, when he had wounded her so deeply that she had almost packed a bag.

Hope had said, "How do I look?" once too often in a 24 hour period and David had finally looked up from grading papers without a trace of humor and had threatened to cane her if she ever uttered the phrase in his presence again. After which he delivered a merciless lecture on her shallowness and self-absorption that had left her in tears.

But as she was pulling luggage out of the closet he stood in the doorway of their bedroom, in his shirtsleeves, his arms folded and with a look on his face that said, "Who do you think you're kidding?"

Hope knew that David was crankier than usual lately because he was quitting smoking, but this didn't make his ultimatum any less cruel. She always said, "How do I look?" That was what she said. She didn't know if she could stop saying it, even if she tried.

"Hope, you're not an airhead. But all too often you leave that impression," David added insult to injury.

"You think so, huh?" Hope had angrily folded knits into her valise.

"A lady doesn't demand compliments," he'd continued to sternly instruct her.

"David, you've said quite enough!" But Hope couldn't go on. She sunk on the bed and sobbed. David sat next to her and pulled her into his arms.

"It had to be said," he maintained, though somewhat more softly, winding his hand in her hair and making her meet his eyes. "You should pay attention when I give you good advice."

Hope felt her tummy contract as he squeezed her smooth upper arm for emphasis.

The next thing she knew he was ravishing her, on the bed beside her valise. She wondered, as he drove into her with all the jagged, energetic enthusiasm of a non-smoker, whether he would really have the steely nerve to punish her severely if she slipped and said, "How do I look?" just one more time. Or would he merely glance at her severely, the way he did when he sensed a "How cute is that?" about to spring from her lips. One never knew exactly what he would do, but it was never exactly what she expected.

"Do you think I'm inordinately concerned with my looks?" Hope suddenly asked her beloved captor.

"Every pretty woman likes to look at herself," Michael reassured her. "And you're one of the prettiest I've ever seen." He paused to rub her bottom. Hope looked at her own face in the mirror while he performed this service for her. She could feel him rubbing her bottom, but her bunched skirt and nylon petticoat obscured anything explicit from her view, which made it doubly erotic. Presently her lace-frilled panties were pulled off and he ordered her to open her thighs by slapping her in between them.

167

"But why suggest sex?" he wondered aloud, spanking her. "When there are so many innocent ways in which I can appease your restless urges along with some of mine."

In the end, she received and was amply satisfied by a vigorous spanking and double digital penetration that very nearly approximated sex, due to the length of his fingers.

"But what do you get out of it?" she said as she was setting herself to rights before departing.

"I'll relive our scene in my mind and derive inspiration from it."

"It seemed as though you had a hard-on while I was across your lap. Can't I see it?" Hope teased.

"Maybe next time," he conceded, slapping her venturing hand on the back of the wrist. "Now behave."

Michael insisted on driving her home though she made him let her out of the car on the road a short distance from the gravel path leading to the cottage.

"You were doing a session, were you?" David had read her brief note on an empty stomach, which had made him cross. A few moments later however, he had found his dinner under a cloth, which had almost tamed his bad mood by the time Hope returned home.

She saw him sitting at the kitchen table and still not smoking.

"Was that all right?" she asked directly.

"Who'd you see?"

"A new person. Highly recommended by Laura."

"Oh?"

"He's an former cop, but totally sweet, being in the scene. I believe he's a freelance writer now. Or maybe he installs security systems."

"What did he bring you for allowance?"

"One-fifty," she admitted with a blush.

"You went out dressed like that for one-fifty?"

Hope shrugged, steeling herself for his next volley.

"Why are you being so nice to this ex-cop?" David snapped.

"Well he's a regular at the bookstore, an extremely pleasant gentleman and he is in the scene."

"How old?"

"Around your age, I guess. Maybe even 40!"

"That old, huh? What's he look like?"

"He's cute," Hope admitted.

"Yeah, I figured, what with the hundred and fifty figure," David remarked, turning back to the Saturday puzzle, but adding, "I expect you'll want to change."

Hope went to exchange her stiff finery for an accessible blue satin gown set, along with a pair of marabou trimmed high heeled satin slippers dyed to match.

Pulling the gown and robe up to view her already well-punished bottom in the wardrobe mirror Hope glimpsed the dark pink coloration that mantled her otherwise creamy cheeks. David too would soon observe how thoroughly she had been spanked by Michael Flagg.

"Was it so wrong of me to give a nice man club rates?" she asked, coming back to him with her hair down, which she hoped still had the power to melt him.

"You tell me."

"Tell you what?" Hope poured herself a cup of coffee.

"Why you blush so painfully whenever you mention the nice man."

"Damn it, David!" Hope sat down at the table with her coffee, sugar and milk.

"What?"

"Okay, I was bad."

They looked at each other.

"I thought so!" David sprang to his feet. "You're in love, aren't you?"

"No!"

"Yes, you are."

"I love only you, my darling!"

"You just said you were bad."

"Nothing happened beyond pure B&D, but only because he was honorable -- not because I was," Hope dramatized.

"Really!" David absorbed this confession with more interest than anger, already under the spell of her radiant beauty in the form sculpting dressing gown. Whatever she did, she'd come home to him.

"David?"

"Uh huh?"

"If Michael brought over a beautiful, submissive young lady, would you consent to an intimate evening of playing with her while M. played with me?"

"What young lady that we know would consent to a thing like that?"

"My friend Susan Ross. She's often told me that she finds you attractive."

"And she'd come over to play just like that?"

"I understand these people in the local scene get together for playing quite frequently."

"You really want to play with him again, don't you? But you don't want to have to take his money to do it."

"No. I want to take his money too," Hope assured David.

"Liar."

"David, I thought about you the entire time."

"Yeah, I'll bet!" David went for the cigarette that wasn't there and so went for the whiskey instead. Hope sighed.

"Hope, get in here," David called from the bedroom. He had started a fire in the bedroom hearth. Their honeymoon cottage had everything but space to recommend it. But they enjoyed being close.

They sat side by side on the bed, he pulling on his shot glass, she leaning her head on his shoulder.

"So, if I understand this correctly, you would have gone to bed with your client, but for his restraint?"

"I'm sorry."

"I thought you never had sex with your clients."

"I don't normally. But I've been attracted to former-detective Flagg for at least the last two weeks. I'd even been contemplating having an affair with him. But when I found out he was one of us, I just changed the affair to a session. Which turned out to be all he wanted in the first place."

David looked at her and said, "You're not endearing yourself to me with this admission."

"David, I can't help it! I'm only 26. I haven't had all that many adventures, not counting the club, and most of those gentlemen were not the stuff that dreams are made on. Then suddenly I'm here in Random Point, surrounded by cool players! You don't realize it but I fight off enormous temptations every day just to return home in time to prepare dinner!"

"Tell me about them." David leaned away from her and folded his arms. Hope arose and put the room between them, going to the window in time to see lightning flash. She thrilled to the succeeding crash of thunder. The rain began to fall in sheets.

"No. You'll only use what I say to punish me."

"Don't you think you deserve to be punished for being unfaithful to me?"

"But I wasn't. I only wanted to be."

"That's even worse."

"Might as well get it over with then," she murmured.

"Bend over the edge of the bed," David told her, filling and draining the shot glass again.

"Why?"

"Just do it."

"But not the strap?" she pleaded, draping her lithe form over the edge of the bed, her bottom towards the hearth.

"Why not the strap?" he sat down beside her and stroked her silk charmeuse covered bottom jutting over the edge of the bed. Hope shivered at the lightness of his touch. Then she turned to see him lifting the hem of her skirt. "I see the pinkness hasn't faded," he commented.

"I told you all he did was spank me."

"I'll bet that's not all he did."

"Why do you say that?"

"I'm sure he spread your legs," said David, separating her thighs, "and noticed how wet you'd become. After that, it's anyone's guess what happened." David pressed his fingertips against Hope's softly fleeced pubic mound, then slipped the middle one into the moist, pink slit that divided it. Hope caught her breath at the gentle intrusion. Twice in one night!

She merely glanced at him over one shoulder, which allowed her to display her delightful upper profile.

"I expect he probed this area thoroughly also, since my wife is such a slut!" David pressed his thumb against her anus.

"Maybe he did, but that's absolutely as far as it went!"

"Oh gee, I'm impressed. All he did was take your pussy and bottom!"

"I wouldn't call it taking."

"I'm sure you wouldn't."

David got up and went to the pine toy chest to find a paddle and small flogger.

"Up on all fours, Hope."

"Why?" she asked, getting up on her knees.

"I'm going to let you off easy."

"Really?" Hope sat back on her heels, allowing the satin gown to fall back down and cover her charms.

"That's right. I'm only going to punish the parts I can see throb."

Hope went limp at the threat and David was easily able to arrange her with her head and bosom resting on the bed, her back slightly arched, her knees wide apart and her bottom uppermost. This position effectively split her cheeks and spread her vulva for him.

He began with the soft leather flogger, lightly fanning her between her cheeks, then carefully aiming to sting her anus with its lash tips. It was a whip specifically designed for the dainty discipline of small or sensitive places. David also plied it against her labia. She twisted, groaned and squirmed, but always arched back to present her spread bottom to him in the prettiest way. Her willingness to receive such attentions betrayed her deep enjoyment of his skills.

By and by it faintly started to sting. But Hope was floating in a certain place. She felt everything keenly but nothing unpleasantly. The humiliation of having her bottom hole whipped almost brought tears to her eyes, but the thrill of the sensation was sublime. The same thing happened when he spanked her Venus Mound with his hand. When Hope was a girl, reading her first Grove Press novels, pussy whipping was described as a cruel and terrifying torment. Since then she had learned the pleasure to be had from such attentions when deftly applied.

To ease her back David slipped one arm under her tummy to support her, but continued lightly spanking her vulnerable, well spread charms until he could see her glisten with excitement.

That was the moment he knew it was proper to take her. She was already in position. He simply got behind her and unzipped. After which penetrating his wife to the hilt was the work of two seconds. He pulled her up by the waist back into the all fours position they had started with to take her forcefully from behind. With the wooden paddle close at hand, he was able to inspire her to move her slender hips in the rhythm that best suited his thrusts. Every time he tapped her on the right cheek or left with the paddle she would catch her breath in surprise. Then he'd hear a belated "Ow!"

At one point he struck her too hard with the little wooden paddle! She cried out and put her hand back to protect her bottom from more punishment, him still in her. But he caught her wrist, pinned it to her waist and casually continued deeply penetrating his wife, the paddle at the ready to administer more discipline as needed. He saw a pink imprint rise on her paler pink skin from the swat she had complained of, and smiled. It wasn't as if she didn't deserve it, thought David righteously, enjoying his husbandly privileges.

Two weeks later they were knocking on the door of the Cliff House, to which Susan Ross had invited them for dinner. The house belonged to Anthony Newton, but when he was away, as was often the case, it was at the disposal of Susan and her sister Laura. Since Anthony was expected within the week, Dennis had been sent ahead with Susan to see to all the details that pleased his employer. Therefore it was he who opened the door to Hope and David, took their outer garments and led them to the downstairs sitting room, which contained a marble fireplace, and gleaming teak wet bar, behind which Dennis immediately stationed himself to appease the new guests' thirst.

Susan Ross came forward to meet them, pulling Michael Flagg with her by the hand. The girls embraced and the men shook hands. David was handed a whiskey and soda at light speed to help him cope with the first impression made by Michael Flagg. Susan proved an immediate distraction, however, overwhelming him with a simple, sincere declaration of how glad she was to meet him in these circumstances and how much she'd longed to play with him from the moment they had first been introduced months before.

"Really!" David couldn't help but turn his full attention to the youthful heartbreaker, her petite form that day clad in a demure navy wool dress, her honey blonde hair loose and wavy down her back and her tiny feet in t-strap heels.

"I'm yours to command."

"Did you wear that outfit because I'm a prep school teacher?"

"Not really," she laughed.

"It's very Gigi."

"I thought you might like that."

"I do," David nodded, draining his drink and beginning to feel as though he'd won the spanking lottery as a direct result of marrying Hope. He looked at her across the room beginning a game of billiards with Michael Flagg and felt a jolt of real emotion for her thoughtfulness. No woman had ever gone to the trouble of delivering another charming girl into his arms for corporal punishment before and the gesture made him feel like an indulged child on Christmas morning. Susan Ross was not merely beautiful, she was clever, charming and herself the mistress of an enormously powerful man. What, David wondered, had he done to deserve such largesse? But when he noted Hope bending over to make her shot, in the shortest wool cashmere dress he'd ever seen, perched on 4" heels, David remembered that she was partially doing this to assuage her own guilty conscience!

"David!" Susan stamped her tiny foot. "You will not moon at Hope while I am offering myself to you!"

"I'm sorry. I was just thinking of something," he impulsively took her hand and rubbed it against his cheek before kissing it and returning it to her, "but believe me, I'm anything but insensible to your charms."

"Dennis, Mr. Lawrence is ready for a refill." Susan grabbed David's glass the instant it was empty. Dennis obeyed but not blithely. He was jealous of Mr. Lawrence, whom he sensed would be offered treasures that evening that, in the manservant's opinion, he could not possibly deserve. And yet, ardent goddess worshipper that he was, Dennis could not help but become violently distracted by Hope's stunningly shot feet as they lightly trod the thick morocco green carpet.

"Dennis and I worked on dinner all afternoon," Susan confided, smiling at her lover's personal assistant, who had adored her since she was nineteen. "Dennis did most of the work," she amended, " but I inspired him."

"What are we having?"

"Stuffed Cornish game hens, wild rice, vegetable polonaise and cranberry-orange relish. And don't worry, we've got lots of Cornish game hens."

"I can't get over the fact that this is all happening because Hope wants an excuse to play with Michael again," David disclosed with mild incredulity.

"David, how can you? Haven't I just said I've been dreaming about you? Consider it a serendipitous cross-pollination. Hope may have been a little naughty, but look at you. According to my friend, you personify a species of male alley cat. I understand you spanked a female counselor at Braemar for several months last year. And Hope also said you caned a girl who had a crush on you."

"It wasn't much of a caning."

"I like not much of a caning."

"I don't know, Susan. You seem too sweet to spank. What reason could I possibly have for disciplining a nice girl like you?"

Susan merely smiled and slightly blushed. She found him so attractive that she couldn't help but impulsively hug him. David found Susan in his arms a not unpleasant thing.

"Don't you feel that we should get this unpleasant duty over before dinner?" he ventured, now tempted to kiss her.

"You're so right!" Susan cried. "I detest being spanked after dinner! Let's go up to my room for a half hour or so." She took David by the hand, calling over her shoulder, "Dennis, bring the whiskey and a fresh glass up, please?"

"You're going away?" Hope straightened up at the pool table.

"We're just running away to my room for a half hour until dinner is ready."

"That's a plan," Hope readily agreed, looking at Michael for approval.

"Sure. We'll just finish our game," he smiled at Susan and David as they departed. As soon as their footsteps were heard treading the stairs Michael dropped his cue and swept her into his arms.

"I've been thinking about what you said," Michael told her, turning her to face the billiards table and bending her over it.

"What I said, Michael?"

"About your being a free spirit and there being no good reason why I shouldn't take you."

Hope was stunned to hear a foil wrapper tear and a zipper come down.

"Michael, what are you doing? You can't do this here!" Hope protested in a whisper as she felt his huge erection nudge against the back of her heather blue sheath dress, which he quickly raised. Her shiny, smoky blue stretch body slip, clung to her slim buttocks like a second skin. He pulled up the skirt of the tight foundation garment with great delicacy considering the speed with which the task was accomplished. Then he encountered the unexpected obstacle of pantyhose!

"Pantyhose? You're wearing pantyhose? To a spanking date? How dare you?" He spanked the offending garment briskly four or five times, but was much more interested in dispensing with them than warming them. Hope felt bitterly humiliated when he roughly yanked down the extremely fine, real silk pantyhose from Italy, which she had gone all the way to Bartlett's in Woodbridge to purchase, as though they were a pair of woolly long johns. Tears filled her eyes in an instant and a painful lump filled her throat. Had she erred so greatly? Or was he a Neanderthal? Did not her legs look past perfect in the exquisite eighty-dollar tights? Or were they really such a gross annoyance?

"No," she murmured, squirming away from him. "I won't let you have me. You don't deserve to now!" Then Hope put her head on the pool table and sobbed.

"Oh my god, what...what's the matter?" Michael turned her around.

"I'd rather die than tell you!" she cried, pulling her pantyhose carefully back up. It seemed that all was well. She felt no tears or runs. Her heartbeat slowed and she swallowed her next sob.

"What the hell is going on?"

"I need a drink."

"What do you want?"

"Rum and coke. Fast!"

Hope composed herself while Michael went over to the bar to make her drink. Happily Dennis was still out of the room delivering the tray to Susan and David.

"I'm sorry," she admitted with a blush as he handed her the cocktail. "You did something that upset me, but I'm sure it's entirely neurotic of me to react the way I did."

Michael let her finish half the drink, while now and then stroking her hair before saying a word. Finally he murmured, "I was way out of line coming onto you like that. Especially if it seemed in any way disrespectful. It's just that I'm finding you increasingly irresistible. Will you forgive me?"

"It wasn't that. I liked that."

"Then, what made you cry?"

"You hate my tights."

"Your tights?"

"My pantyhose. They're real silk from Milan. You practically ripped them off. It made me feel both unattractive and fetishistically inept! And it's all so unfair. Every other time I've ever played I've worn stockings. With seams! But I thought I'd let you sample the best in fine hosiery. And you see what happened." Hope bit her lip to stop herself from bursting into tears again at the insult remembered.

Now it was Michael's turn to redden, and he did so as only one of Celtic extraction can do. Hope was alarmed at the change.

"God, I'm so sorry!" he declared in a guilt stricken rush.

"It's okay. I'm getting over it now," she assured him, gulping her drink and feeling much better for it. "I'm the one who should apologize. I showed bad judgment in wearing tights." The humility in

Hope's demeanor caused Michael's anxiety to vanish and his excitement to instantly revive.

"You're such a girl," he teased, to kid her out of her unsettled mood. "First thing I should spank you for is being so sensitive!" She accepted this judgment with soft acquiescence, almost returning to normal after having her say and seeing him so honestly contrite.

Taking her by the arm he led her to a large, armless chair, whereupon he turned her over his knee.

"Perfectionist that you are, Hope Lawrence, I'm sure you'll never wear these again, since I've probably snagged them at the least, so I might as well experience this silk of Milan to the full," he explained, raising her skirt and under slip to reveal her somewhat shiny, sheer mesh, cocoa beige, seamed tights. These were worn over her bare skin instead of panties and he could see the fine cream of that pearly flesh with great clarity thorough the silk knit. "Oh, Hope, dear, you were so right. These are lovely." At the risk of snagging them with his weight lifter's calloused hands, he ran his right palm lightly across the slim ovals of her bottom. He began to pat her bottom lightly, then a little harder and finally to spank her in earnest.

Hope wanted to cry, "You see how well the pink shows through the silk mesh?" But she was too gentle a soul to double damn her dominant. It was enough that he now realized his mistake and was willing to handsomely acknowledge it! Hope wriggled across his big lap and he held her fast. His hands were huge and warmed a bottom quickly. Somehow the silk mesh seemed to hold in the heat and at the same time chafe her tender flesh. Hope suddenly remembered that one of the reasons she so seldom got spanked in pantyhose was that the mesh grill made the spanking seem to hurt more!

"Okay, I'm ready now!" she was inspired to cry.

"Ready?"

"What you suggested before. I'll kneel up on this chair and you can take me from behind, just like you said."

Michael didn't need to be asked twice. Quickly he arranged her in the perfect position and proceeded as before. This time Hope carefully lowered her own tights to mid thigh before presenting herself to him. But she was not prepared for his grandeur and the first thrust nearly made her cry out.

"My god, take it easy with that thing!" she pleaded. He withdrew an inch or two and lightly pistoned it in and out. "You put a condom on, right?"

"I'm glad you can't feel it."

"Can you?"

"Yes, but who cares. I'm fucking you." Michael reached around to cradle Hope's flat tummy against his hand, working his fingers down to rest against her clit and took her with decided restraint. "I'll bet you could take the whole thing anally," he teased.

"Go to hell!" she laughed. To punish her he thrust in hard, which caused her to instantly gasp. Meanwhile he pressed his palm against her lower abdomen so deftly as to give her ten or a dozen mini-climaxes. At length he withdrew.

"They could come back any minute," he reminded her, disposing of the evidence of their tryst in his jacket pocket.

"Yes, we should have gone into a room with a lock on the door," she agreed, setting her clothes to rights and checking her watch. "At least a half hour has passed. They'll be back any second."

"Right," Michael strode back to the bar, "to be continued, I hope."

Hope smiled in mild acquiescence, proud of how well she had managed her first extra-marital affair.

About the Author

In Random Point, everything is linked to spanking and this is true for the author of the Shadow Lane novels as well. Eve Howard has been writing and producing spanking erotica since the 1980's, when she began freelancing for one of California's largest fetish magazine publishers. While editing *Spank Hard* magazine (as Lizzie Bennett) in 1985, she was discovered by the video producer Nu-West and offered a chance to perform in spanking videos. In 1986 she published the first Shadow Lane story and the following year formed the video production company Shadow Lane with her partner Tony Elka. The Shadow Lane novel series, originally published by Eve in serial form in her magazine *Stand Corrected*, was brought out in paperback volumes by Blue Moon books beginning in 1992. There are nine titles in the Shadow Lane series and Eve is currently working on Volume 10.

Since 1988, Eve has written, directed and produced over 140 spanking videos, the vast majority featuring the same male-spanks-female dynamic portrayed in her novels. Female-friendly and designed to make people feel good, rather than guilty, about being into spanking, Eve suggests an irreverent alternative to the all or nothing B&D subculture portrayed in such beloved classics as *The Story of O*. Many spanking fans have discovered the real life spanking scene by following the same patterns of social networking as described in the Shadow Lane novels. And for almost twenty years, Eve's company Shadow Lane has been one of the primary social organs of the real life spanking scene. She lives with her husband Tony and three cats in Las Vegas.

Reader Reviews about the Shadow Lane Series

"I've become addicted to the "Random Point" series so much that I can't wait until the next chapter. I've ordered the first two Shadow Lane volumes and have re-read them over and over. I never tire of them. Eve is the only person I know who can make an enema sexy."

"I discovered Shadow Lane about a month ago via AOL. Prior to that time I thought I could write excellent spanking erotica. Then I ordered, "The Problem with Laura." This is just a note to commend Eve Howard's spectacular talent and to say thanks for an incredible erotic experience."

"I have just completed "Return to Random Point" and decided that I had to write about how much I enjoyed it. I have not been so aroused since reading my first discipline novel many years ago, about a girl raised in England and "coming of age" as I believe they put it. More recently I have enjoyed reading Grant Andrews' My Darling Dominatrix and Ann Rice's "Beauty" series. It seems that women, though, have the right touch when it comes to writing about this subject. Eve, especially, knows how to touch that erotic nerve and bring it to a pure, raw sensuality until one feels that he/she is near bursting with lust."

"I, for one, have always loved (and by loved I mean devoured... breathlessly) Eve Howard's novelettes. To read them... especially when I was just 'coming out'... was to feel completely validated. I truly identified with each and every heroine; the feisty, sassy ones, the shy, demure ultra 'subby' ones... the young ones, and the more mature. I loved the gentle yet firm "taken in hand" nature of the romantic variety of spanking D's that Eve always incorporated into the stories. I loved that the plots were not complicated... but, feasible nonetheless. I loved the depictions of sexual escapades after many of the spanking interludes. I appreciated that the girls were cherished and adored by the affably rogue-ish gents... that the submitting was willing and desired... that it wasn't like 'rape.'

I like the settings... having grown up in New England and living here almost my whole life. I LOVED the idea of the bookstore (which I always find sexy). Then and now. I could cite many passages too, but I fear I've rambled enough. Eve was/is always my favorite spanking author."